MAGGIE ROSE

By: Jonathan Masters

Preview Edition

Constance,

   Your inspiring service to
our youth will ripple through
generations.

   Blessings,
   J.

Maggie Rose
ISBN-13: 978-1981288151
©opyright 2018
All right reserved
Wider Lens Productions – Chicago

www.widerlensproductions.com

For all my Firecrackers. The girls with brightly colored hair and a matching personality who, despite the great burden they carry, find a way to carry on and make others smile during the process.

For all the dreamers, hustlers, and grinders doing work at the local library. Over half this book was written in a public library. Never stop reaching far to change your stars.

For the Matchless Creator of the Universe and Personal Savior God who will never burden us beyond what we can bear and will always be the Hope for the hopeless.

Foreword

While developing such devastating stories as *The Throwaway Kids* and *Maggie Rose*, I realized how essential a clearly defined sense of hope is. As a teacher for incarcerated, mentally-ill, traumatized, and abused kids, if I ever felt there wasn't at least a glimmer of light at the end of each kid's journey, my job would be nearly impossible.

So, I came to appreciate, early in the writing process, how important it was to give Maggie a sanctuary and place for respite. Growing up, my place was my grandparent's house. I infamously declared, "There are no rules at Grandma's house," and it really did feel that way. We got to watch an endless reel of cartoons and eat more grease and sugar than a young body should be capable of handling. In fact, Grandma pushed the limits at a Cubs game by feeding me so many Twizzlers, nachos, hotdogs, sodas, and funnel cakes that my five-year-old self puked purple onto the kid in front of me before the second inning had started.

Besides spoiling me rotten, my grandparents were my biggest fans. My grandpa was at every childhood sporting contest, and they both were at every play, recital, and graduation. I'd be hard-pressed to name a significant event where their shadow wasn't cast.

To survive her journey, I knew Maggie would need something similar to identify with during times of great struggle.   Who better to guide Maggie through trepidation than my own grandparents?

To honor them and to give Maggie an anchor, I distilled some of my own memorable feelings and experiences to create a backdrop for this story.

We love you Grandma Rosie.

We miss you Grandpa Bill.

Your legacies run deeper and reach farther than you could ever imagine.

Hint: The format of the following fiction can seem shrouding at times. All will be revealed in time. For those who don't prefer suspense, simply read the last chapter to create clarity.

October 9, 2009 11:30 PM

The first time I ever stole from my mother was two weeks before my fourteenth birthday. The last couple of years, she took me to the mall and handed me a wad of cash saying, "go nuts," while she mumbled about taking sips from a flask that she'd hide in her purse.

I figured I had this money coming to me anyway, and I could pay her back by not going for broke on my birthday like I usually did.

I had just gotten back from school and my mom was still sleeping. She works the graveyard shift, so I had a fifty-fifty shot of finding her passed out when I get home, especially when she decides to get liquored-up and argue with the morning news like she did that morning.

I could see her purse on the dresser from the hallway. It was wide open with money and makeup mixed about. My sixteen-year-old boyfriend, Justin, had asked me to bring some cash to pitch in for booze that night. Normally, he would cover me, but this time he was strapped for cash from the insurance payments on his T-Top Camaro. Just thinking about how that car purred and hugged curves makes me wet.

Why do you keep fiddling with your phone? Are you recording this?

You perve.

Whatever; it's your time.

Anyway, I make it all the way across the room and pinch a twenty from her purse. When I pivot to make my escape, the floor makes this deafening creak, and I freeze. Like, I'm not breathing and neither is my mom. I don't know how long that went on, but it felt like forever.

Finally, she took this big inhale, half-snore, and I busted out of there.

I was so hyped. I almost ate a whole bag of chips while watching music videos until Justin picked me up at six. We met up with the rest of the crew at a playground behind the liquor store we liked to go to. Justin's buddy Zeek had this lame fake ID that I'm sure the clerk knew about, but a sale is a sale, right? And, Zeek usually walked out with at least fifty bucks worth of booze.

It was Friday night and Renee's parents had gone to a wedding or something. We teased her that they were gonna grind on each other all night then "make love" in the hotel suite at, like, 10:30 before passing out. We really didn't give a fuck because it gave us a place to party.

Renee was a little jumpy because she was paranoid that her parents would show up or send someone to spy on us. Justin turned on the charm with his crooked smile and put an arm around Renee to share the plan. We'd keep the lights off upstairs and party in the basement. Mellow music kept low, so if anybody did come, we could sneak out the well-window with the booze.

By eight o'clock, Renee was well on her way to being toasted, and we all forgot about the threat of intrusion.

Later, when everyone was good and sloppy, Justin gave me a half-smirk with a tipsy twinkle in his eye and led me to Renee's backyard. There was a hammock that we sat on sideways, so Justin could rock the hammock with his toes.

We passed a bottle of fruity wine and stared at the stars. Nothing was really said. I'd giggle a little which prompted Justin to kiss my forehead. After a while, the stars got bigger and were, like, rimmed with rainbows as I faded into oblivion.

I woke up shivering, and my legs were wet. I was still drunk, but I could feel the hangover had started which didn't help as I tried to figure out where the fuck I was. I tried to stand up off the grass, but I found my pants were wrapped around my knees. The moon was full, and I could see my underwear were dark and wet.

At first, I thought I had my period. But, I remembered that treat had ended five days ago. I buttoned my pants and tried to get back into Renee's house. The lights were off, and the door was locked.

I went through the gate on the side of the house and couldn't find Justin's car. So, I thought it best to walk the two or so miles back to my apartment in the dead of night.

The liquor was still keeping me warm, but I had to blow on my hands and rub my arms a couple times. At first, I was mad as hell. I replayed over and over in my mind how badly I was going to bitch out Justin's dumb ass.

But, as I could see my apartment building, I realized Justin had just broke up with me. He screwed me and left. He was probably freaked out about my virgin vagina blood all over his dick.

Even to my naïve, middle school brain, the message was becoming pretty clear. You don't do that to someone you're hoping to see again.

When I got in our place, I stripped down and took the hottest shower I could stand. Despite washing and washing, I couldn't get the sticky feeling out from between my legs.

When the water went cold, I stayed in as long as I could stand it, hoping the freeze would numb the pain.

I put my bloody clothes in two grocery bags and stuffed them under my bed. I put on a t-shirt, sweats, and a hoody with the hood pulled over my head and shivered myself to sleep under the blankets.

That was my first time.

Memorable, huh?

Is this getting you off, Doc?

You want anything else from me because our time's almost up?

October 13, 2009 12:35 AM

My full name is Rosa Margarita Gonzalez. When I tell people my name is Margarita, they think it's like a fake, "stripper" name or something. My mom named me Rosa as the Mexican equivalent of my grandmother's name, Roselyn.

I think Mom was trying to be clever or romantic with the middle name. Mom didn't think it practical to hide the fact that she got knocked up by some Cholo at an all-night taqueria or something. "Tequila" would have been a bit much, so mom kept it classy with "Margarita" as a wink and a nod to how trashed she was when I happened.

Mom gave me His last name thinking that a one-night stand would stick it out. To his credit, he took my mom on a couple dates she tells me. He didn't show up on my birth day and has been scarce ever since.

Since we've lived on and off with my grandparents for as long as I can remember, the adults decided "Rosa" was too close to "Grandma Rosie." So, my mom started calling me Margarita, even trying to roll her "R's" like a true gringo.

My grandfather had a difficult time acknowledging my bastard origins, so being the Irishman that he is, decided to call me "Maggie Rose." Though he refused to put up with an inch of my mom's bullshit, Grandpa Bill always said my name with tenderness. Every time he said, "Maggie Rose," it felt like I was his and his alone.

My dutiful grandmother fell in line calling me "Maggie," and my mom respected the rent and did her best to remember to call me "Maggie" while grandpa was around. I think Mom intentionally slipped up when it was just her and Gram to make Rosie blush.

October 19, 2009 11:55 PM

Well . . . since this is gonna be a pretty regular thing, Doc, I feel like I'll just go on and open up to you. Do me a favor and steer the ship a little, will ya? My mind tends to wander weird fuckin places sometimes.

My childhood was pretty enchanted, you know. Despite being fatherless, I never really missed out because of my grandpa. Some of my earliest memories are of him pushing me on the swings.

Looking back, I think I could tell something was off because of the "underdogs."

Some kid next to me asked his mom to give him an "underdog." She counted down and ran under the swing, pushing the kid really high. The kid giggled and snorted and kicked, and I thought, "that must be fun." So, I asked Gramps to give me the ole heave ho.

He counted down but ran next to the swing with one hand on my back because he wasn't quite fast enough to make it under. A few times, he was still pushing when gravity wanted to bring me back down. I had to hang on for dear life because he would have slid my ass right off that swing.

I never did stop asking him for swings, though. Grandpa Bill was rickety in the joints, but he had strength in his hands from years as a plumber. I think we both liked the swings because it was easy to bond. Playing hide and seek was never gonna happen with his enormous frame.

I had to go easy on the old fart, like my mom did. But, I think its cause I liked him. My mom just needed a roof.

October 23, 2009 11:15 PM

Doc, man . . . we gotta see if we can get a discount rate with as much as I'm seeing you. You know, like a "friends and family thing." Otherwise, this bill is gonna get price-ey.

Mom and Grams hated each other. I think that's how Mom got knocked up in the first place.

At one point, I think Mom was the apple of Grandpa's eye. But, that ended sometime before my mom was kicked out of the house before graduating high school.

She still graduated. A fact which she uses to motivate my studies.

I don't think it had anything to do with the value of school or getting a good job. I think she finished solely because she had spent the better part of four years being dragged through classes, and the thought of that time being a waste eeked her across the finish line. That and she wanted to stick it to my grandpa a little. To kinda show she wasn't a total fuck up.

Despite her shortcomings, high school graduation is a must for me. She dreamily thinks I'll go to college or something, too.

I don't know, I suppose the books beat hooking or something.

Yeah, Mom and Grams would go at it four or five times a year. These big brawls would get my grandpa's attention, and in the heat of the moment, Mom wasn't having the, "While your under my roof, young lady," speech. She'd tell off Gramps and slam the door behind her.

When I was really young, my grandma would try to console me directly after the carnage. She'd get right to baking and fill the house with some type of sugary goodness that she'd pepper me with throughout the days. Grandpa would always bring home a princess movie from the rental place.

Life was good for a couple of days. Then my mom would wander back in like a stray dog, looking all strung out and exhausted as shit.

The house got quiet and tense for the hours and days to follow. But, the wounds would callous with time, and we'd go back to the unspoken roles we were supposed to follow.

October 27, 2009 11:40 PM

I remember one particular, nuclear event when my mom took me with her on a storm out. I think Mom knew that taking me from Grandma and Grandpa would really cut deep, and maybe next time, they wouldn't fuck with her so much.

We stayed at her friend "Jerry's" house. Jerry's wife, Charlene, did her best to keep me in front of cartoons as much as she could. The only rule at Jerry's house was that I couldn't play outside. Charlene and Mom made that very clear. After the lecture, I didn't see much of Mom.

The place was a dump and smelled like shit. There were people lying around on pads and blankets in every room. I even saw two people going at it in a bedroom. They were buck naked, no blankets, and left the door flung open for like everyone and God to see.

I hated going to the bathroom because there was almost always vomit around the toilet. If I was lucky, I didn't have to be the one to wipe down the seat before I'd go pee.

There was plenty of food, though. A guy named Trent would bring in a huge, black, plastic bag full of all kinds of bagels a couple times a week. I always got strawberry cream cheese if it was around. Sometimes, all they had was butter.

After a couple of days, a squad of police came busting through both sides of the house. Everyone was scrambling, and some dude knocked me into the couch, and I scurried around the side and wedged next to a chair to avoid the chaos.

The police used zip ties and laid everyone on their stomachs like dominoes. I was given a blanket and sat in the back of a police car. I kept craning my head to see where my mom was on the ground.

A sweet, pretty medic talked to me in a singsong way to keep me from freaking out. But, as we loaded into the back of the ambulance, her partner had to help strap me down because I wouldn't stop squirming and calling out, "I want my mommy!"

None of the belly-fish wriggled to indicate my mom had heard me, and they slammed the doors as we sped off.

At the hospital, they undid the harness around my chest and legs. A balding, beer-bellied doctor asked me a whole bunch of questions about my mom and Jerry's house and how long we had been there and what was going on. I told him what I knew which wasn't much.

While we were talking, I saw my mom through the window. She tried to come busting in, but some cop caught her collar and dragged her to the ground. I went running out of the door, but a couple of dudes in white grabbed my arms and brought me back in the room. They asked the doctor if they should strap me to the bed, and Doc sternly asked me, "Is that necessary, Margarita?"

I didn't give a FUCK! I wanted my mom, man.

The two goons turned me on my belly and put these padded handcuffs on me and tied them to the bed. They took away my pillow and left me writhing from side to side crying for my mommy.

Evidently, I gassed myself out because when I woke up, the shackles were loosened and the doctor was sitting there with a clipboard and his glasses at the end of his nose.

He told me that my mom couldn't see me right now. He said my grandparents were there, but it would be a couple hours before they could take me home. He asked me how I was "feeling."

I'd been living at a crack-house, or some shit, for a week. I thought my mom was in jail. I'm in the hospital, chained down, and not able to go near the people I love.

I'M REALLY FUCKING GREAT, DOC!!!

My grandparents took me home in the hospital gown they gave me and a loose pair of scrub pants. They probably thought it would be traumatizing to take me home in the filth I'd been wearing since I was dragged out of their house.

The next day, Grandpa went to the local grammar school, St. Elizabeth's, and signed me up for school. I started the next week.

My grandparents got me the uniform and a backpack full of supplies. They even took a picture as I walked into the school. All while my mom was in a court-mandated, rehab facility.

November 1, 2009 11:09 PM

My grandpa demanded that my mom allow them to change my name to "Margaret Rose Hennessy." But, because his custody was temporary, it didn't get far.

I think my mom kept me "Margarita" out of spite. Just to let my grandparents know who was in charge of me.

Mom finished her rehab and made a triumphant return. My grandparents were on edge for days waiting to see what Mom would do next.

Slowly, we got back to a normal, cease-fire pattern.

Nobody wanted to disturb the peace. So, I think for the longest time on record, nobody rocked the boat.

November 4, 2009 11:59 PM

Man, Doc. It's startin to get cold. I'm glad you called and picked me up because I was about to pack it in for the night. I thInk my knees arc blue.

I didn't go to school with any of the other kids on our street. They all went to the public school. They told me that going to a Catholic School was "old school."

I found out that my grandfather sent Mom to St. Elizabeth's because, at the time, a lot of Europeans were arriving in our part of the city. Because my grandparents were third generation, they didn't want their kids being slowed down by a fresh crop of foreign speakers.

I think, in a pinch, Grandpa just went with what he knew and enrolled me in Catholic School too. Either that or he put me there to avoid the "negro-blacks" and the "Mex-E-cans" as he called them.

Either way, look at where a wholesome education got me.

November 6, 2009 12:47 AM

My friends at Grandpa Bill's house were Jimmy, a boy two years younger than me, Hassan, an Indian kid a grade behind me, and John and Willy. John was two years younger than me, and his baby brother was like five years younger than me, but he shadowed us ever since he could waddle in diapers.

Being around all boys, we played a lot of sports. Whiffle ball, basketball, and soccer were the favorites. The only one I was any good at was soccer.

Sometimes we'd ride bikes, and on rare occasions, we'd rollerblade. My grandparents got me rollerblades for Christmas one year. And, I can remember strapping them on and racing through the street after dinner.

Mom and the rest of the family walked along with me and yelled if I'd get too far ahead of them.

Anyway, we couldn't rollerblade a lot because only Jimmy and John had skates, and Jimmy sucked at it.

On rainy days or when it was cold, we'd play this game called "dark tag" in John and Willy's basement. Basically, the person who was "it" had to go upstairs and count to fifteen. Everyone would hide around the basement. Then, the "it" person would come down and try to find us with all the lights out. The first person who was found was the new "it." The last person to be caught won that round.

We never kept any official tally of who won the most. The person who thought they won the most games was always a little cocky at the end of the game. Once, Jimmy and John got into a shouting and shoving match because they both thought they'd won.

Willy didn't really get it. Most of the time he'd jump out first and say "boo." Since he couldn't really be "it," the next person found would glumly trudge the steps to the kitchen. It pissed everybody off when Willy would "boo" us and then reveal where someone else was. I think he had a crush on me because he'd say, "Geegee's over there; over there," repeating the last syllable of my name twice. If John was it, he'd make sure to spot someone else before me and even let me win sometimes.

He was a gentleman like that.

The best spot, by far, to hide was in the furnace room. Almost every game, someone was hiding in there. It was awesome because there were no windows to the outside in that room, so absolutely no light. Combine that with the fact that the person who was "it" was coming from the bright upstairs and would be relatively blinded in that room, and the utility room made for an ideal hiding spot.

Because we were so little, at least one of us could shimmy between the water heater and furnace to hide behind everything. So, blind-man "it" would have to fumble around the slop sink and reach through one of three different openings to tag someone. We were always scared to touch the furnace or water tank because we thought we'd get burned. Especially when the furnace was roaring and you could see the fire through the grates.

If the "it" person missed, they'd sometimes grab pink insulation and be grossed out like it was spider webs or something.

I'd loved this spot because several times I'd been nimble enough to dodge the groping hand, and one time, they even had to call for me after giving up the search because it took so long.

For some reason, John and his brother Willy got on this, "I see London; I see France," kick. The group of boys would find a reason to sing the song, and then one of them would tell me I had to show them my underpants.

At first, this made me really uncomfortable. It would take multiple boys badgering me with these gross, googley eyes before I gave in.

After a while, when I realized they weren't going to give it up, I just pulled my pants down and up quickly before they could complete the song.

The game kinda lost its luster when little Willy kept repeating the song and then would try to pull my pants down. John put a public end to my peep shows at that point.

What John really wanted was his own private party. He found me in the furnace room one day and sang the song to me. He stepped outside the door, so a little light would shine in, and I pulled my pants down and up. Then, John blocked me from leaving, saying I did it too fast. When I held my pants down so he could get a good look, he told me to pull them lower. I got freaked out and slid past him to get out of the closet.

John didn't give up. He'd regularly hide in that room when he knew I was "it." When I found him, he'd sing the song and tell me to pull my pants "all the way down."

When I had gotten used to this drill, John asked me to pull down my underpants. I said no, but John blocked me and pleaded, "Just a quick peek." I grabbed the band of my panties with both hands and quickly flashed him my snatch.

John let me go that day, but "liar, liar pants on fire," became our new, private game. In order to put the fire out in my pants, I had to pull my pants and undies, "all the way down." He would leer a couple of seconds and then tell me to pull them back up.

I think John got spooked out of it when he asked me to turn around one day. He'd already had his fill of my front, so he wanted to check the goods out around back. Willy surprised him with a "boo," and John covered the doorway long enough for me to cover up.

I think John knew it was wrong. He just couldn't help himself.

I stopped hanging around with those boys around second grade. They weren't around as much because of sports teams. I was even playing soccer on my own girls' team and many social events were planned during our practices.

Me and the neighborhood boys just kinda grew apart, even though we still lived next to each other.

I don't know how much John being a pervert played into it. I think I just avoided the boys on cloudy and cold days for a while.

Why, good doctor! Is that liquor I smell on your breath? I do believe you might just be smashed this evening.

My mom moved us into the pigeon shit-fested apartment complex she lives in today towards the end of 3rd grade. I think the walls are brick, but for all anyone can tell, they've been covered completely in varying shades of white.

This place is barely a long walk away from Grandma and Grandpa's, but I think Mom and Grandpa had finally had just about enough of each other. My mom was holding down a steady job as a breakfast and lunch waitress which meant she would be home when I got back from school.

This was probably the heyday of mine and Mom's relationship. She was relatively sober when I was around, and we'd go to parks and the library and shit.

Thinking we were chums, I'd often ask her, "Can I do this?" or, "Can we do that?" For which, she'd reply, "That's too expensive," and, "We don't have the money right now, Honey."

I'm pretty sure she tracked down most of the free opportunities in our town and made a solid go of being a parent for a while.

To be sure, she'd still go on benders from time to time. I'd see her getting caked up with makeup like a whore and smelling like a berry patch. She'd tell me I was spending the night at Grandma's.

My grandparents would deliver me home after lunch the next day, and Mom would do her best to hide the effects of the previous night's poisoning. But, as soon as the door shut, she'd promptly pop in a movie for me and pass out. I'd be left to fend for dinner on my own.

Most times, she'd be over the worst of it when I arrived. Though, I did get to hear my fair share of fireworks from the bathroom over cartoons and crunchy chips.

November 14, 2009 11:35 PM

Mom let me finish St. Elizabeth's my third grade year while we moved, but then I switched to Marie Currie Elementary for fourth grade. My grandparents protested, saying they would pay for the tuition, but I could tell my mom wanted to be freed of anything they could possibly hold over her head.

I kept the peace by reassuring my grandparents that I wanted to switch because my soccer friends went to Marie Currie.

I don't know if I knew the difference at that point between Marie Curie and St. Elizabeth's. For the most part, all kids listened to the teacher and followed the rules. Recess was by far more rowdy, but we'd always rein it in when the monitor stopped talking to her buddies and started walking toward us.

We were all still terrified of the dreaded call home. I never did give the school a reason to call Mom. I think the idea of the trouble I'd get in was magnified in my little brain.

Things are just simpler like that when you're younger.

I still saw Grandma and Grandpa pretty frequently because Mom had to regularly do a weekend morning shift. I think she could have gotten the time off, but everybody knew how busy the diner got and how good that could be for me and Mom.

My grandparents went from raising me to spoiling me. Just as it should be.

They'd kept my room the same, and Grandma and I would bake some sort of goodies that I'd get to eat there and even take some home. Grandpa was still good for the princess movies, even though I was getting too old for that.

The trips to the park were getting less frequent. I really didn't want to be seen alone with just my grandpa, and I think the years of wear were starting to take a toll on old Gramps. Standing up had become a production where Grandpa would have to lean back and rush forward, throwing his arms out, to ride the momentum out of a chair. Otherwise, he'd kind of scooch to the edge of the chair and push off both of his knees to get up. It was slow going, but Grandpa Bill would always chuckle at his success. I think that was to reassure me that everything was okay.

Grandpa Bill loved teaching me card games during our drearier days. He taught me cribbage, kings in the corner, pinochle, bridge and rummy. My grandma would join us when necessary, but most times, she preferred kibitzing around the house either cleaning or doing cook prep.

Since, "they aren't teaching you much at public school," Grandpa would use these times to really challenge me. He'd teach me tricks by beating up on me and revealing how he had done it later. It didn't take me long to get a hang of the games and start having fun, but I rarely won.

On the special occasions when I got the best of Grandpa Bill, I'd immediately quit games for the day to savor my victory for as long as possible. I think this really rankled the old fart because he'd go after me extra hard during our following sessions.

November 17, 2009 11:52 PM

You caught me in a chipper mood, Doc.

It's kinda been a bitch of a week, so I helped myself to some of Shelly's booze.

I've been pretty good recently, so I thought I'd earned it.

The rum paired nicely with a couple of pills, and I am currently feeling no pain.

November 18, 2009 7:45 AM

Ugh, Doc. You're a regular champ; you know that, buddy.

I've woken up in some weird places after a bender, but this definitely makes the top of the list. You've got some swanky digs; you know that.

Ahhhmmmm, what smells so heavenly? Doc, you made breakfast? You shouldn't have.

This is incredible, Doc. I've been to my fair share of diners, so don't take it lightly when I say you're quite the cook.

Can you top me off with a little coffee there?

How did I get into that bedroom anyways? The ride over is a little foggy, and I don't remember much after mumbling through your door.

You carried me. You stud! I know I'm a skinny little bitch, but damn Doc, you went all Paul Bunion and shit.

I think I just got to celebrating too early, Doc. You know today is my birthday.

I kinda started thinking about life; you know? This in not quite the fairy tale I thought I'd be in at this point.

Who's Shelly? Oh, I mentioned her last night. We working girls have a rule about not divulging people's real identities and shit. It's kind of a code thing.

Shelly and a couple of the other girls I hang with crash in this shitty one-bedroom, second-hand apartment. There're no beds, so we're not tempted to bring work home, but plenty of couches.

We all share clothes and food and stuff. We like crashing the thrift stores for good deals on clothes. We dumpster-dive behind high end bakeries and grocery stores to fill up our cupboards.

No one is possessive over food because most of it was free. We keep a quiet tally of who had to buy what and try not to pig out on someone else's shit.

There hasn't been a fight so far. It's kinda a regular commune minus the nuns.

You want me to stay here? Why?

Doc, I'm flattered, but we got a good thing going here. I really don't want to fuck that up, and up close I'm kind of a hot mess.

I'll tell you what; let me think about it? I need to clear the pounding in my head before I make any life-altering decisions. Alright?

November 21, 2009 6:30 PM

I'll give you this, Doc; you are persistent. How did you get Stephon to let you know where I live?

No, really. I'm curious. He'd never give up one of his girls just because you charmed him.

Oh, you're gonna be bashful now, are ya? Gonna play that, "a lady never tells," game with me, huh? I thought we were passed all that, Doc. I thought we'd developed a, what-do-you-call-it . . . rapport?

Alright. Well I can't say I'm not grateful. This is a palace compared to my dump. But, I'll have you know, I'm gonna earn every sent of my rent. Margarita is no mooch.

November 22, 2009 7:30 AM

What can I say, Doc? I'm the daughter of a waitress. I learned me how to cook a mean omelet and grits.

On days I didn't have school, Mom would bring me to her diner.

Usually, I'd keep myself busy in the corner reading or coloring. I was whisper-whipped into understanding the importance of blending in with the scenery.

The owner was this warship of an old Polish lady who was never without a scowl. I called her The Vulture because of her bony frame and long nose and because she'd hover around people she was about to peck on.

She'd do her best to perform a cordial "thank you" when customers would settle their receipts. But, years of carrying around that mean mug had worn it deep.

The cook made his way out by me during one of the slow spots. TJ, short for Travis Junior, was the son of a preacher-man, but TJ had lost his way. A repeat fuckup, like yours truly, TJ had become a short-order cook because it "steadied his hands."

I think good ole TJ appreciated what kindred spirits we were and turned me into his apprentice when no one was looking. TJ got me a stool, so I could watch him, and he could talk at me instead of mumbling just to himself.

When there were only a couple customers in the diner, TJ would give me simple orders and let me attempt to put them together. TJ clapped and barked good naturedly to hurry me up. He'd always say, "Yo momma's tips is a waitin, Girly," and tap his wrist where a watch should have been.

Anyway, I owed you a breakfast.

I'm gonna wander to the store today while you're gone. You have, like, zero food in this house, Doc.

Tonight, we dine on Grandma's specialty, chicken pot pie.

November 29, 2009 6:45 PM

Even though I no longer attended St. Elizabeth's, Mom still made me attend religious school on Wednesday nights. Well . . . I wouldn't say *she* made me attend so much as Grandpa Bill did.

Grandpa Bill insisted on signing me up for "Catechism" right away when Mom signed me out of St. Elizabeth's. Grandma and Grandpa would get me all gussied up, and we'd attend Mass every other Sunday when Mom was at the diner.

Church was really important to them.

Grandpa Bill was even a deacon or something. Grandma Rosie and I would sit in the second pew, and Grandpa would walk in with the priest and sit in front of us in the special "reserved" pew. He got to do one of the readings and served Communion, like, every Sunday.

Every Wednesday after school, Grandpa Bill would pick me up around 5:30 and take me to some fast food place for dinner. He'd quiz me on what I was supposed to know for church while I dipped French fries in my milkshake.

These were the only times Grandpa got stern with me. If I couldn't put together some solid responses to his queries, he'd get all flustered and fill in the blanks, saying, "Maggie, you've got to know this stuff. It's very important."

Once, I completely blanked and told Gramps quite a tall tail on the spot based on bits I'd put together from

31

previous sessions. I thought I had him going until his palm smacked the table. "Maggie Rose! Are you really going to sit across this table, look me in the eye, and lie to me about God?"

I don't think the blood left my cheeks until long after Grandpa had dropped me off at home, and I was tucked in bed.

I told my mom I didn't want to go to church anymore. But, Mom said it was "something I should do," so I could "be a good person."

I could tell Mom wasn't a huge fan of church either seeing as she never took me. I didn't push too hard because I figured religious school was just like school school, and Mom would lecture me about the importance of paying attention, so I "wouldn't end up like" her.

I didn't and still don't really believe in God. But, I believed in Grandpa Bill.

Grandpa was always so sweet to me. I know he did his best to fill in for the dad I didn't have, so I gave him a break here and there. I know I didn't really fit well into anybody's plans.

To see such raw anger come out of him and directed at me, it left a mark, man. I studied church like crazy for, like, a solid six months.

After seeing how important God had seemed to become to me, Grandpa laid off a little bit.

Hey Doc, speaking of church and shit, I think we missed Thanksgiving.

I noticed you mumbling about the house and watching football.

It looked like you hit it hard and hit it good. I'm all about a good wasted day, but it didn't seem like you were all that happy.

Had I known the day, I would have planned better. Sorry. I'll make sure to get us a proper feast for Christmas.

Hey Doc . . . don't you have any family or anything to spend the holidays with?

December 1, 2009 6:15 PM

I think it's sad, but safe, to say that TJ was my best friend in, like, fourth and fifth grade.

Girls are all about their looks, and that period saw many of my so called "friends" getting into high fashion.

The thing with girls is they like to layer. I think something about having to remove all those layers really builds the suspense for men. Something about two different colored skinny straps sticking out of a sweater, and man, you can get them boys salivating like pups.

I know you know what I'm talkin about, Doc.

I don't think it was about fashion or warmth. I think it's just wrapping. If done right, wrapping can magnify what's getting presented.

My friends would show up to school with like three or four shirts on, a blingy belt, some neckware or jewelry, and bracelets and shit. I've never even had my ears properly pierced.

My mom took me to some little girl's jewelry store in the mall the morning of my First Communion to get my ears pierced. There was a swivel chair just outside the door with a "$15 piercings" sign on it. Some teenage twat used a gun to shoot a little gold stud through each of my ears. It fuckin hurt, Doc. Man, it fuckin hurt.

I couldn't stop rubbing my ears during the whole ceremony. I can't remember what anyone was talking about because the throbbing drowned out my hearing. I thought I'd have permanent damage.

My grandma shot a million pictures outside the church, and I tried not to wince with the flash because the "pop" sound of the flash reminded me of that twat's ear gun.

The next day, I woke up and my ears were beet red and, like, twice their usual size. All day I could hear my heartbeat.

My mom tried putting some cotton ball medicine on it, but that made it worse, like both sides of my face were on fire.

The next day, Mom and I probably woke the neighbors with her trying to pull these fucking things out and me screaming, sobbing, and moaning for a solid twenty minutes.

I haven't had my ears pierced since. I've heard "beauty is pain," but, for fuck's sake Doc, there's gotta be limits.

Mom couldn't afford all those layers for me. When things would start getting tight, Mom would take me to the Goodwill and make me get clothes with "room to grow."

I constantly went from a giant that was about to tear right through the top of its shirt to being flooded and hoping my pants didn't wash away in public.

My retarded fashion sense was all well and good at soccer practice, but I found that at school when these girls wanted the boys to notice their peacock feathers, no one wanted to stand next to me.

December 4, 2009 7:45 PM

I'd regularly save my big life question for when I saw TJ. Being a preacher's son, he knew all the right things to say. He'd also traveled a rough road in life, so he'd also give me solid reasons to follow that advice.

When I told TJ I didn't need no schoolin because I wanted to be a cook like him, TJ had a clever response. "Miss Margarita, a cook's a fine thing to be, a fine thing, BUT the thing about your ed-ju-ma-cation is it gives you options. See, you can still be a cook, and a damn good one at that because of all this quality trainin you be gettin, BUT you can also do a whole lot of other things."

"Like what?" I'd asked him. I wasn't trying to get smart with TJ, but my mama was a waitress, Grandpa Bill was a plumber, Grandma Rosie mended dresses at a cleaners, and my best friend was a cook. Out of all my available options, cook seemed the best thing for me to do.

TJ took a good while to think about it, and I thought he was gonna give me this list, but instead he said, "When I got locked up, I had got this lawyer. He was a young nigga like me, but he always had on this slick suit, shined shoes, polished brief case, and he'd had a couple pairs of fly lookin two hundred dolla sunglasses. Man, I'd like to do what he did."

Thinking about being a lawyer really made me pay attention in school because lawyers needed a lot of school and needed to read a ton of thick books. Grandpa Bill even gave me these legal thriller paperbacks he'd read.

Nobody really told me or them that a little girl shouldn't be reading about murder and scandal and sex. Most of that stuff grossed me out anyway. I really read them to understand what lawyers did. And, it seemed really exciting.

So from that point on, I'd decided I'd like to be a lawyer.

TJ told me pay attention in church because church was filled with "good people." He said nobody in life can make it on their own. We need family and church folk and the like to help us along the way.

I remember he'd said, "When you and yo mama moved into that partment, who moved the couch and bed and dressas?" I told him that my grandpa had hired movers as a gift. Flustered by the extravagance of hired help, TJ ran with his point none-the-less, "See, life is juss plain easier when you gots peoples surround you to help you, Girly."

TJ went on to explain that all that preachin and congregatin got people to love on each other. He put it like this; "Church is about creatin a community that helps those when they needs it. Helpin gives the person doin the helpin and the person givin the help hope. And that's the bess thing we can have in this life, Girly. Hope."

I kinda understood love as a bunch of different services, you know. The more we performed these services, the more we loved someone.

My grandma loved me because she'd bake me cookies and stuff and feed me.

My grandpa loved me because he wanted to keep me safe, teach me, and help me grow and learn.

Mama loved me because she busted her ass working and put her own fun on hold at times because she wanted to support me and raise me right.

I don't know how I loved them back, though. I think by trying to do what they taught me and told me to do was my part.

And, I knew when I had done it just by looking in their eyes. Some of my best and worst memories can be summed up by how the people I loved looked at me in those moments.

December 11, 2009 8:55 PM

I know that look, Doc.

Margarita's gotta EARN her keep.

I know; I know. I just thought you brought me in here to talk is all.

Just sit right there and relax. Ma Ma's got to work for her living.

December 16, 2009 6:25 PM

Diana Long was, like, the Queen Bee of our 5th grade class. She was a scrappy, broke kid like me, but her mom understood the importance of fashion.

Diana wore the layers like everyone else, but you could tell her layers weren't as expensive. Don't get me wrong, her shit was first-wear, department store quality.

But, the majority of her clothes weren't mall quality like the most popular girls.

Diana turned the tables when she sprouted a set of knockers quicker than anybody else. Even though they weren't much more than a half a tennis ball pushed together by a training bra, she still landed the coolest, most popular boy in our class. This tool named Sean.

The other girls started to huddle around her like the radiation she gave off would pop out their own tits. Boys stared and StArEd and STARED at her cans when they thought no one would notice. Then, the boys either got tongue tied or this goofy, fake, Rico Suavé grin when they were around her like her boobs had melted their brain or something.

I think my rack was just as tantalizing as hers at the time, but I was going through another flooded fashion faze, and mom said she didn't believe in training bras. She told me, "I'll get you a real bra when you get a real pair of knockers."

In any case, Diana lost some of her luster when a rumor started to spread that she stuffed her bra with tissues. Sean and another mean girl would even make jokes about it while passing a tissue box back and forth and offering it to other kids and Diana.

The joking stopped when Diana beat Mindy Dubois's ass for holding up a stretched out roll of toilet paper right in front of her shirt while we were playing softball in gym class. Diana slapped Mindy across the face and then, like, tackled her. As the boys watched these two bitches kicking up dust, I couldn't tell if they wanted to cheer the fight or cream their pants.

When Diana got back from suspension, I'd stared at her boobs day after day to see if they'd change size or shape. One day I thought the left one was slightly bigger than the right, but after Diana came back from a potty break, all was balanced and adjusted.

I gave up the quest to solve this mystery at the end of the year, and to this day, I just can't be sure. I don't know why it still bothers me.

Whether she had it or not, she worked it. I'm not gonna hate.

December 19, 2009 7:05 PM

By the end of fifth grade, I was pretty much a loner. Even though I had some mad soccer skills, the popular girls on my team wouldn't even look at me because of my unfortunate fashion sense. They acted like ugly was contagious and made sure never to get too close to me.

I think I had started getting friends who were boys because I was athletic and aggressive like them. They loved to win, and so did I. I wasn't even picked last among the boys. Man, it was shitty for the boys who got picked after me, but fuck them, man; I came to play.

Mom's money troubles ensured that I dressed more like the boys too.

And, I think boys liked hanging out with me because they could practice their talking to girls on me. I think I was like the warm up. Boys would chum up to the non-threatening Tomboy to get up the courage to talk to their bombshell.

Man, those dorky movies about the homely girl having a kinda personality that charms the heartthrob guy are total bullshit!

Toward the end of the year, we had this field day. I did really well at all the contests, and near the end, I was ranked the best girl in school by a solid mile and fourth total behind two sixth grade boys and Sean from my grade.

One of my last events was this apple bob. The point was to dive head first into a bucket and fish out five apples with your teeth the fastest.

Most of these prissy bitches refused to participate, afraid to smudge their makeup or hair. My fashion gave me no reason to back away from this challenge. My only goal in life at that moment was to beat these boys and get me some playground bragging rights.

And I did. I was the fastest apple bobber in the school. I did so well that it moved me into second place, and I even got a blue ribbon on a podium and shit.

The problem was that my ravenous bobbing soaked me from my head almost to my knees. Wearing a faded white, grunge-metal band T-shirt that day was an extra poor choice because for the last hour of school, including the awards ceremony and pictures, my little pink ladies wouldn't stop peeking out.

I kept pulling at my shirt, but like a strong magnet, my shirt would just suck right back to my poked out nips.

I wasn't made aware of how bad the situation was until the weekend had passed. After returning to school, several boys had hollered "Margrrrrita! Yeow; yeow!"

I thought I was getting the praise I deserved for whoopin every boy in the school except for one sixth grader. Diana, with a snide, little, shitty grin, pointed out to me that they were applauding the peep show I gave them from the podium.

I was horrified. I literally walked around with a hunched back and a textbook pulled to my chest for the last two days of school.

Needless to say, I had zero friends for that summer. The girls were disgusted with me because the homely girl stole all the boys' attention with her bangin boobs. And, the boys were too chicken shit to ever talk to me again.

When I tried to show up at the local park to play soccer, every boy there just gawked at me and wiped at their mouths occasionally to hide the drool. We barely got through picking sides. Every boy wanted to guard me up close when the ball came my way, trying to rub up against me or something. The game was shit because all eyes were on my shirt, hoping they'd notice a bounce.

December 24, 2009 6:20 PM

Merry Christmas, Doc! I know I muffed Thanksgiving, so I thought we'd do it up right. We got ham, greens, mashed potatoes, dumplings, and cranberries straight from the can.

You know you can call me Charlie. I think we're passed the whole doctor/patient thing.

Well, Doc, I mean Charlie, add that to the long line of miracles I've had in my life recently.

Cheers to you, Charlie!

I'm not all that religious, Dah—Charlie. But, I thought we should have a proper blessing.

Dear God, thank you for the best year I've had in a long ass time. Sorry.

Thank you for Charlie and this food and this house and this whole situation. I've got it really good here.

Good food, good meat, good God let's eat. Amen.

Can you pass me a little more of that Chardonnay, Duh—Charlie?

I'm so glad that you got in contact with your family for the holiday. Don't worry about me. Like I said, this is the best Christmas in recent memory. I haven't got a care in the world. I think I might even wander over to that church across the road over there to sit through a proper Mass.

I just feel lucky, you know, Doc. I mean Charlie.

You just enjoy your relatives. Really take it in, you know. Family is a fickle thing, man, but if it's good, there's nothing better. So, be your charming self, and have some fun for Christ's sake.

We've got enough leftovers to eat for days. I think I'll get good and shnockered after church and watch a Christmas movie marathon.

If you're party's a bust, I can get you caught up quick, and we can waste the holiday away under the covers.

December 28, 2009 10:35 AM

I'm sorry, Charlie. I just need to take a walk somewhere . . .

Today is the day my Grandpa Bill died.

I was in sixth grade, and we were on break from school. It had snowed all Christmas day, a real winter wonderland you know. I had always wanted to go skiing, and for Christmas, Grandma Rosie and Grandpa Bill had gotten me a snappy purple and white winter coat with a ski-lift ticket in the pocket.

I was so stoked to go, man. I'd been all bundled up, for like 30 minutes, before we were supposed to leave.

Evidently, Grandma was running behind or something. My mom called over all snippy, like, to bitch them out. I think she was just jealous that Grandma and Grandpa had never taken her skiing.

Grandpa decided to walk over to pick me up and walk me back to their house, so Rosie and Mom wouldn't keep going at it. Everybody knew I could make the walk a couple a blocks by myself, but Grandpa liked being a gentleman and escorting his little lady.

Grandpa Bill never made it.

My mom paced the kitchen chain smoking into the stove vent, muttering swears and curses about being late to her shift and losing our rent. I bounced on my knees looking over the back of the couch out the front windows towards Grandpa's street. I was goofily singing all the wrong words to Christmas songs with my coat and boots on, ready to go.

I was watching for Grandpa. I knew if I ran out to meet him, he'd only suffer my mom's furious lashing from a distance.

Instead, an ambulance came roaring past our window. It turned the corner toward Grandpa's house and disappeared.

It took a second to come into focus, but I could see the flashing lights reflecting off the windows and walls of buildings, like it had stopped in the middle of the street or something.

I don't know what possessed me, but I took off out of our house and went running down the street. I made it just in time to see Grandpa Bill getting loaded into the back. He had this oxygen mask over his face and reached out a heavy arm for me when they shut the doors.

A jackass paramedic shoved me down when I tried to get in and told me to go tell my mom they were taking him to Heritage Hospital.

I paced the waiting room for hours with my coat and boots still on. I think I figured, if I didn't take them off, then Grandpa Bill would still take me skiing and everything would be okay.

My grandma came out sniveling with a tissue to her red, swelled eyes. A guy in scrubs had an arm around her, and my mom fell to the floor, screaming, "No! Oh God, NOOO!" while sobbing and pounding the tile.

I just stood there.

I just kept thinking, "What am I going to do without you?"

I don't know how long I was there. I don't remember leaving.

Sorry to unload this on you, Charlie. I just need to take a walk and clear my head.

I think I'm gonna head down to the cemetery to see him, you know.

I go there sometimes and stare at his name to calm my fears.

The letters W-I-L-L-I-A-M H-E-N-N-E-S-S-Y just bring back the sense of peace I had when Grandpa Bill would put an arm around me and pull me into his side on the couch while we watched movies.

I think I just need to visit him, today of all days. Pay my respects, you know.

January 3, 2010 6:50 PM

The start of sixth grade was really uneventful.

I was nervous as shit after not seeing anybody from school for most of the summer. I kinda freaked out the morning of the first day and didn't go.

This was the first of many times that I'd intentionally skipped out on school.

In my scaredy sixth grade brain, I figured that was it. I've dropped out of school now, and there's no going back.

It was actually Diana of all people who convinced me to come back. That bitch called me and left a message on our answering machine saying, "Margarita. You know school started today don't you? Well, I hope you're not dead or something. Come to school tomorrow, will ya? Or don't. I don't care. *click*"

A real peach that Diana Dearie. She'd make some miserable fuck so lucky one day, he'll wish he were dead.

Evidently, all that worry was in my head because a bunch of people I thought hated me came running up to me when I stepped off the bus.

They all had like a million questions. But then, they'd tell me their answer to their own questions before I could get a word out.

I was kinda thrown off. I thought I was gonna have to walk into school and have to fight a bitch to keep people from fucking with me all year long. But, the mystery of the disappeared Margarita had only been fueled by me not showing up to school the first day.

Apparently, my knockers had earned me some notoriety. The jealous bitches routine turned into my budding bosoms being everybody's bestest buddies.

The boys were downright scared stiff by me. Things had progressed to the point I needed a little more support. And with last year's tees being a little form fitting, it was plain to see the outline of what I had going on, and the boys didn't know how to handle it.

I never could get in a good game of soccer going. The boys were terrified to touch me. I think my newfound fun-bags left them with bouncing boners, and I don't know how it is for men, but it hurts like a mothafucker to run without the girls tucked back.

January 6, 2010 6:50 PM

I found my new place in sixth grade social society among the giggling gaggle of girls who would meander just out of earshot of the boys and whisper and point and cackle like they were clever or something.

Looking back, I think that shit was moronic as hell. But, this was like the first time I'd ever had a group and fit in and shit.

I was even supposed to meet Brittany and Heather at the ski mountain the day my grandpa died. A bunch of the girls called my house for days afterwards. My teacher even orchestrated a card making marathon because I was gone the first two days back from winter break to go to the funeral.

This not showing up to school shit really built up the Margarita image, man. I was like a total badass rock star in these girls' minds. And since the blood rushed away from boys brains when I was around, the boys just followed the girls cue and made me the queen of sixth grade.

It was a good life, you know. We were at the top of the mountain at Marie Currie Elementary.

To teach us responsibility and shit, sixth graders got these volunteer monitoring positions, complete with these nylon, orange vests.

We were put to work checking bathroom passes during break times, getting everybody lined up to enter and leave the school. And, because we had to get to our posts early, I got to put my backpack at the front of the bus line and got the one-seater backseat of the bus every day.

That was, like, the shit back then. Sitting sideways, stretching your legs across the aisle.

It really was a baller time, Chuck.

January 12, 2010 7:15 PM

I remember thinking in the days between when Grandpa Bill died and when he was buried that it might have been better if he just died there in the snow.

There's something romantic about it, you know. Stumbling and sliding to the ground, cushioned by the beautiful, white, pure snow. It would be almost angelic; the soul leaving the body surrounded by that bright glow.

Instead, they had to pump him full of drugs and tubes and shit.

And then, they pushed my Grandma Rosie out of the room to blearing beeps and calling codes and trying to shock Grandpa back to life and shit.

That's fucked up.

I know they were just trying to help. But, that's just fucked up.

Grandpa Bill deserved better.

January 16, 2010 6:50 PM

The wake was uncomfortable as shit, man.

We had to go in early to help set up. Grandma Rosie's church had made a boatload of dishes of food and shit. Evidently, if you're Polish, that means you eat when you're happy, eat when you're sad, and just eat all the times in between.

I'm lucky I'm not, like, 400 pounds or something, surviving in that family.

It was a good thing Grandma was a little oompa loompa because I don't think she ate for weeks after Grandpa kicked it. She lost like a ton of weight and her neck and arm skin began to sag and wobble and shit.

My Uncle Larry flew in from San Francisco. He was like some washed-out, stoner, hippy, fuckup or something, so Grandpa didn't like to have him around.

Grandpa was proud to have served in the Navy during Vietnam, and sonny-boy never found a bottle of booze he didn't want to dip his toe into and eventually drown in. I mean you couldn't find two more different guys.

Grandma Rosie would convince Grandpa to buy Uncle Larry a plane ticket home every two or three years to reunite with the family. By the second or third night of the trip, Larry would get nice and shitty and tell everybody what their fucking problem was.

Grandpa Bill was probably equally as shitty, but you couldn't tell because of how composed he kept himself. Grandpa would repeat the song from memory of Larry's long list of let downs.

The evening would end in a "Fuuuuck YOU!" and slammed door with shitty Larry storming off down the block. Larry would find a couch to crash on for a couple of days and return the morning of his flight for awkward apologies over breakfast, and Grandma Rosie would drive him to the airport.

This cycle had repeated itself over and over until I was in fourth grade.

The first couple of times, I was terrified. Mom or Grandma would hug my head and hurry me to my room where they thought I'd be out of earshot.

I wasn't.

By fourth grade, this had become a sort of holiday tradition. So, I watched Uncle Larry and Grandpa Bill hurl insults at each other over potatoes and gravy.

Grandpa Bill was my boy, you know, so I'd smile or laugh when he'd gotten Larry good.

Uncle Larry didn't find this funny towards the end of the night and turned to me to say, "What are you laughing at, you little bastard bitch?"

Grandpa Bill launched his chair into the wall and moved faster than I'd ever seen him move to grab Larry by the collar and lift him, shove him, and even cock back like he was going to slug him a couple of times. Grandpa chased Larry out of the house and stood on the porch to scream obscenities at him as Larry fleed down the block not sure what the fuck had just happened.

I tried to hide my giggly grin for the rest of the night because I knew no one else found this the least bit funny. But, come on. Grandpa Bill, my boy, had gotten down for his number one ho, you know. I was flyin high, man.

That ended quick when we got home to find Uncle Larry on our couch.

In her infinite wisdom, my mothering older sister of a mom gave Larry a key knowing he'd storm out at some point. She thought she was doing the right thing, not letting Larry freeze. But, I think a little fresh air would cool his drunk, arrogant ass off a little bit.

I think he could tell I wasn't having any of his bullshit either because for the next two days he wouldn't even look at me so much as talk to me.

When we all ate, Mom would have these conversations with him as if I weren't even there. When their shit got played out, Mom would turn to me, and we'd pretend Larry wasn't there.

Grandma Rosie picked up Larry and drove him straight to the airport that time. That was the last time Grandpa had seen Larry, and I don't think either called the other to apologize.

January 19, 2010 8:05 PM

Uncle Larry was like the bell of the fuckin ball at the wake, man. He was smilin and schmoozin and fuckin yucking it up with every family member and friend that came his way.

I could swear he was happy that Grandpa Bill bit it. I didn't even see him visit the casket once.

When they buried Grandpa Bill, the Navy sent out a trumpeter to play their bedtime song and fold up a flag and give it to Grandma Rosie.

Uncle Larry played the part perfectly, looking all hunched with his arm around Grandma. He even offered to carry the flag while Grandma hooked one of his arms, when I know for a fact Larry would have rather wiped his ass with that flag.

Grandpa wasn't exactly buried either. Grandma had bought two stones in a wall to stuff his and her body into at the end.

The whole process didn't really sit right with me.

I mean I thought you were supposed to stand in the rain under umbrellas and shit and hear a boring preacher mumble to you "all was well" and "Grandpa Bill was in heaven" and shit. The preacher wouldn't fool anyone because he'd be so boring and unconvincing that I'm sure at the end of the day he'd look himself in the mirror and be like, "What the fuck am I even doing here?"

Instead, everyone followed Grandma Rosie out of the little Chapel at the cemetery, and we went across town to eat sausage and potatoes and shit for lunch.

I mean . . . everyone just left Grandpa Bill there. Cold and alone.

That really bothered me. He deserved more than that, you know?

January 26, 2010 7:40 PM

As I said, my social life picked up after Grandpa Bill's funeral. I'm pretty sure my little family crisis was the most traumatizing thing to happen in any of our little worlds, and that changes your view of people, you know.

Even the bitches who wanted to hate on me had to put themselves in check because they wouldn't know what to do if they lost their Nana or their Papi.

Diana's parents split in fourth grade and finalized their divorce when we were in fifth grade. Everyone had to feel sorry for her, but her parents were still alive, and it meant two birthdays and two Christmases and shit. That's when Diana's hotness level raised a few notches. Each parent spoiled her with shopping excursions in an attempt to buy her love.

I think that little bitch even learned to play Mom and Dad's hatred off each other. She'd explain that she'd got her knew backpack or shoes or coat because she told one or the other that the mom or dad wouldn't buy it for her. The parents jumped at the opportunity to one-up each other, and Diana was swimmin in swag.

Grandma Rosie came into a shit-ton of money when Grandpa kicked it. Evidently, Grandpa had a couple of different accounts and investments and shit, and he left Grandma flush with cash.

I think Grandma knew how hard I took Grandpa dying, and I think her and my mom felt a little salty because

56

their argument sent him out in the cold in the first place. So, they both decided the best way to heal everybody's wounds was a little retail therapy.

A couple of weeks after the funeral, Mom interrupts my lounging away a Saturday by telling me we're gonna take a little drive. I was laying with my head dangling off the couch up-side-down and barely paying attention to a rerun marathon of some teeny-bopper drama shit. So, I thought, "What the fuck? I'm game."

We headed straight to my grandmother's house, and she comes bouncing down the porch with her purse clutched to her chest with both hands and a goofy, little kid grin plastered across her face. Mom and Grandma thought it would be fun to surprise me with our little shopping adventure.

We hit the mall, and Grandma put four one-hundred dollar bills in my hand. I nearly peed my pants, Charlie. I clutched the money with a death grip and almost punched a hole in my pocket, shoving it as deep as I could get it to go into my jeans.

I didn't get a chance to think about the shopping spree because I was so terrified of losing the wad that sat in my pocket. I'd get lulled into forgetting the money was there, then I'd panic and pat my leg to make sure it was still shoved deep. I even had to go to the bathroom and lock myself in a stall to pull it out and count it to make sure it was all still there.

Only when I had piled and folded the bills down twice, nice and neat, and shoved them tight in that little hideaway tight pocket of my jeans, could I then concentrate on the task of finally beautifying Margarita.

I burned through that money quick, man. Now, I know why my mom never took me shopping at the mall. After buying a new coat and a pair of sweet kicks, I barely had enough money for a full outfit, with complementing panties and bra of course.

I think I wore right through that first prissy outfit because I would make sure my mom washed it constantly, so I could wear it to school twice a week, every week.

I slowed down my wear and tear after a couple of more shopping sprees when my wardrobe began to fill in. By that point, my first outfit was played out. At least, I figured I better give the boys something else to gawk at.

Mom and Grandma wanted to show what a functional family we had by taking me on these trips to the mall every month or so. We really didn't see each other much outside of these excursions. I guess their simmering hatred for each other was kept in check by them cooing over how cute I looked.

I think these trips really did help me get over Grandpa's death. He always made me feel like a princess. He protected me. Regardless of how shitty I feel, it still relaxes me to think about sitting next to that gigantic man and having him pull me in close, tight, secure.

Shopping with Grandma helped me because she was the only person Grandpa adored more than me. I think he lived for making each of us smile, and I think Grandma Rosie lived for my smiles after Grandpa Bill passed. I made sure to do it up for her and create a show to make Grandma happy and to keep the trips coming. I don't think my acting was too off base because that spring was like the highlight of my life, Charlie.

February 1, 2010 6:25 PM

My newfound fashion only heightened my rule over the sixth grade social classes. The ugly duckling who everybody knew would one day be a swan finally got to spread her wings a little.

Those clothes really made a difference, man. I not only looked damn good, but I knew I looked damn good. The clothes gave me this cocky swagger, and I became a little bit of a bitch too.

I started experimenting with flirting. I knew the boys brains melted around me, so I tested a couple of seductive voices asking for shit like a pencil or some paper or to pass me a book.

When I knew boys were watching, I'd really accentuate my lips by wrapping them around the food I was eating. Or, I'd place a pencil between my teeth like I was thinking about something, and when I got some fool's attention, I'd sensually use the edges of my closing mouth to move the pencil to a dangerously dangling position between my lips. Just when it was about to fall out, I'd gently pinch the pencil between thumb and pointer and slowly glide the eraser across my bottom lip, pulling it down as a tease.

At least half the time, boys' jaws would drop open, or they would shake slightly from the tension in their pants. Man, I loved getting them all twisted and goosed up.

Thinking back, when I did seductive shit like that, I thought I was getting a rise out of them because they wanted to kiss me. I really think that's what was in their heads too.

If I walked over and reached down their pants to grab their little pecker, I think each boy would have fainted right out.

Man, what a difference a couple of years can make.

My newfound ownership of being the baddest bitch at Marie Curie divided the girls. I got a gang of girl followers who gawked and giggled at the gullible boys who I led along. They'd recount, in great detail, each of my activities and how the boys reacted, while I smirked over my hoard with approval.

Yeah, that shit happened.

Yeah, I'ma bad bitch.

Diana did not take being dethroned very well. Her click feuded with mine. And, she threatened me on more than one occasion.

I think the power grab went to my head or something because I finally ran right up to her and screamed, "What! Do something, bitch!" I made sure to boob bump her to show her my dominance.

You could hear a pin drop because every single kid on the playground stopped in their tracks and stared at us.

Diana looked shocked. She didn't think I had the backbone to rip her Queen Bee crown off her prissy, blond-streaked head. While she fumbled, I said, "That's what I thought!" and I glowered up and down at her as I walked away.

My posse was a buzz. Those bitches retold that story like eight different times that night. I put on a tough and cocky grin to cover up the fact that I was shitting bricks. I thought Diana was gonna rip my head off and piss down my throat.

The next day, Diana and I kept our distance from each other. Our underlings buzzed back and forth with each other, but the bosses steered clear of trouble.

Things stayed at a tense standstill for the rest of that year. Word would travel from one crew to the other that Diana or I were talking shit about the other. We'd get red and yell insults and make threats inside our own little click which would make its way over to the other gang, but nothing came of it.

I think the stalemate was because both of us were scared shitless to have the other bitch tear out our hair and beat our ass.

February 3, 2010 6:40 PM

My elementary school principal was, like, heartbroken that I wouldn't claim the field day crown at the end of sixth grade. This bitch was all about girl power or some shit and wanted me to be the first girl to have her name added to this stupid fucking plaque that had the winners' names on it dating back to, like, 1964.

Mrs. Schultz even gave me this speech about "women needing strong models" and "girls looked up to me;" I was "an example."

People staring at me was exactly why I wouldn't do that shit, again. I'd had quite enough of that last year and knew there'd be an audience lined up around the block to see my girls jump and jiggle through each and every obstacle.

Fuck that!

Plus, I was out of practice. I'd taken to makeup like a fly to shit. I kept having to wake up earlier and earlier to get ready for school, and I wasn't about to let sweat or movement smudge my new perfection. I had an image to maintain; an adoring audience to keep happy.

I don't know if I could have even done it again. But, I fueled the belief that I could have.

Being too cool to compete is the way to go, Charlie. My minions teased every boy who was tussling for the top position. They'd whine in the most nasally way, "You wouldn't win if Margarita competed," and, "You're just lucky you don't have to be beat by a girl this year," or,

"You better be careful, or Margarita will come and beat all your butts."

Without ever lifting a painted fingernail, I was the undisputed champion of field day.

It's good to be the queen.

February 7, 2010 7:20 PM

Graduation was tits, man! Mom and Grandma fawned over me at the mall to get the most memorable outfit. And, if you ask any of those prepubescent jerkoffs I graduated with, they'd tell you it was unforgettable.

I got this red, spaghetti strap number and a tube-top, push-up bra that gave me the first cleavage I ever had. My growth spurt left me with legs for miles that I accented with a matching pair of red pumps.

In hind sight, a mini was probably a pour choice. I wore a thong so the fabric rubbing against my bum would have the boys bent over to hide their boners. Lucky bastards got more than they bargained for when we first stepped outside the school, and the dress fluttered up.

I'm sure several of my classmates can describe in detail Margarita's dimpled cheeks.

During the punch bowl social in the gym, I didn't have to walk an inch to have my yearbook signed. At several points, the line got to be about five or six people deep.

Several of the boys burned red from ears to ckeeks to neck blotches as they wrote, "Hope to see *more* of you this summer."

Jackasses!

My grandma took me, Mom, and Larry out to a fancy dinner to celebrate the occasion. Grandma even held up her wine glass to toast my accomplishment by saying how proud Grandpa Bill was of me, looking down from heaven and shit.

That really soured my day, Charlie. I couldn't think about how exciting junior high would be or make mental plans for the summer. I couldn't even enjoy the food, even though I was starving, because I was thinking about the empty seat at our table.

That was the first time I realized that every time something good or something bad happened, or just every time we gathered and pretended to be a family, there'd always be an emptiness, a void.

I still feel it now, you know?

He was my hero.

        Now, he's gone.

                And, he's never coming back.

The summer between sixth and seventh grade was all about beach babes in bikinis!

Since we proved ourselves stellar students at graduation, most of the parents gave their darlings a measure of freedom that summer. We used ours to stake our claim to the apartment's swimming pool and clubhouse.

Our routine was to meet at my place around eleven. We'd check each other out to make sure we were all hot shit and adjust accordingly. We'd also get a healthy dose of tanning lotion going and help each other in the hard to reach places.

The point was to tantalize the boys, but if they saw us rubbing each other down with lotion, they'd likely stroke out in the pool and drown. And, we couldn't have that, now could we?

Once we were all glowing, we'd wander down to post up on the lawn chairs with the best sun exposure. The clubhouse had a boom box that we'd tune to 101.4 Hip-Hop Hotlist, and we'd lounge, looking gorgeous to lure the boys over.

Sean had the biggest group of goons. Outside of Sean though, there wasn't a looker in the bunch. They were all scrawny and freckly and pale. Sean was a head taller than all of them and had the makings of a six-pack and some promising dimples on his arms that might become muscles one day.

He made the soon-to-be seventh graders swoon, but I was looking for something better.

The fact that Sean was that bitch Diana's old news really turned me off. His goons tried on more than one occasion to pass messages through my gals to get us together.

During a couple of moments of weakness where I thought the only accessory I was missing was a boyfriend, they almost made it happen. But then, I'd think about Diana's bitchy sneer reminding me that I got her sloppy seconds. I imagined them making out all sucky-face-like when I'd stare at Sean's lips, and it made me gag.

While the boys trounced each other in the water, trying to drown each other for our affections, I coolly peered into the future pool of middle school boys who'd be waiting for Margarita at the end of summer.

February 14, 2010 6:50 PM

Charlie, have I got a night planned for you. For starters, a candlelit steak dinner, with asparagus, mashed potatoes and garlic bread. I poured the good red wine in the decanter to let it breath. And for your viewing pleasure, this little black number I picked up.

Do you know what's special about this dress? It's so silky against my body that I couldn't bring myself to wear any underwear underneath. That'd just ruin all the sensations.

Hold your horses, big boy. I forgot to mention dessert.

I've melted some mouthwatering chocolate that I'll be slowly drizzling over each of us, so we can savor each other for the rest of the night.

February 17, 2010 7:15 PM

I found out that douchebag Sean was an even bigger tool than I'd imagined.

My grandma had given me some summer fun money for graduation, and me and my girl-squad decided to venture from our little apartment pool to the local waterpark one day.

The waterpark situation was not ideal because the lawn chair lounging area was quite a distance away from the actual pool. We'd hoped to be on full display for the boys splashing around. Instead, for several hours, no one dared venture through the divide for fear of coming off too desperate.

When I finally got fed up roasting myself, I decided that we'd paid our money, and we should enjoy a slide or two.

As soon as we stood up, we saw the most disgusting sight. Sean was sitting at the bottom of a lawn chair between the spread legs of a face-down Diana. We saw him caress the bottom of her feet to send a shiver up her as he stared at her jiggling ass. What a player-perve this jackass was.

The rest of his goon-squad were attempting to follow suit, but they weren't as arrogant as their leader. Most of them were twitching next to a girl that shifted uncomfortably as they tried to break the awkward silences. But, the boys' mush brains were too focused on not letting the girls catch them checking out their every nook and cranny, so the conversations were pretty shitty.

I took our gang to the farthest point in the park away from Sean's fawning over Dirty Diana, and we bitched for an hour about what an annoying asshole Sean was for playing both sides.

Right then and there, we made a pact to never give any of those boys an ounce of a second look ever again. If they'd come by our pool, we'd take a walk. If they'd follow us, we'd lock ourselves in my place until the coast was clear.

Those little boys were better than dead to us.

Sean spotted me as he was walking out of the bathroom still tying his shorts. I could tell I surprised him because he dropped one of the strings and the trunks nearly slid off his skinny ass.

As he embarrassedly tried to compose himself, he made his way toward us and did this running leap to splash a wave on me. "When did you get here, Margarita?" he said accusingly, as if I needed his personal invitation to enjoy this pool.

"Long enough to see you rubbing up against Diana, you mongrel." I was done with him, so I turned to swim off and get back to our sunbathing spot.

Sean cut me off, "Come on, Rita. I was just trying to get my boys some action." He smiled as if I would catch his charm and get all warm and gooey for him. I found it disgusting.

"You know Trent likes Lisa. I think they're, like, dating now. And anyway, your girls are too afraid to leave your side to get with my boys."

I was having none of that bullshit. "Screw you, Sean. I thought you liked me."

"I did. I mean; I do. But, how long do you expect a guy to wait. You keep leading me on and brushing me off. Are we going to get together or what, Rita?"

Though his asking me out left a lot to be desired, the look on his face was sincere, and I think he was a little bit hurt that I kept him at arm's length when he clearly thought he had spit some fierce game my way.

"I think I'm good, Sean," I brushed him off because I was honestly thrown off by the genuine affection I could see in his eyes. I was confused by the difference between his uninterested, standoffish demeanor and the tenderness in his eyes at that moment.

It didn't last.

Sean splashed me hard in the face, and the water burned my eyes, "I knew you were a bitch anyway."

Oh shit, Charlie, my blood boiled at this little fuck. "Just run on back to Dirty Diana, Sean! I hope you catch a disease, and your dick falls off, you prick!"

As soon as the words left my lips, I think I stunned myself into silence. I would routinely talk some crazy shit to my gals with a little Latina flare, but never had my assaults landed directly on the person I'd intended to hit.

For Sean's part, his feet melted into the hot concrete. He stood there like a metal statue being slowly heated to a glowing red. It was only when my posse started splashing him and saying, "Yeah, go back to Dirty Diana. You guys deserve each other." My girl Tina came up with the sickest burn, "Dirty Diana and Slimy Sean, a match made for a trailer park." This was a little low, even for me, because it was rumored that Diana's dad had to move to a trailer after the divorce. But man, was I proud of my girls.

As we confidently glided across the pool to triumphantly return to our loungers, I heard my name, "Margarita? Is that you?"

The sun was blinding and the pool was packed, so it took a second before I spotted this blond, bronzed god paddling over to me.

When he arrived, he stood way too close, and I had to stare over his luscious lips to see up into these arctic blue eyes. My ears were still burning from the hate I spewed at Sean, so I couldn't figure out for the life of me why this stunning hunk was offering me shade from the sun. "It's Christian, remember? I was a year ahead of you at Marie Curie. You almost caught up to me at field day. Remember?"

No Christian, I don't. I've been doing my damnedest to forget the degrading details of the day where my boobing for apples gave the entire school a free show of my lady parts. The trauma that followed me around all summer is permanently seared into my memory. How was my Tom-boy, overly competitive, oblivious to boys, fifth grade self supposed to remember a blazing hot hunk like you?

But instead, I said, "Oh yeah. Congratulations on getting your name on the plaque, by the way," as I stared up dumbfounded at this shadowed face with a halo of the sun around it.

"Did you come back and win the whole thing this year. I was rooting for you." Evidently, I did make a competitive impact because Christian was sweating so much as I closed the gap that he picked me out of a crowded pool a year later.

"Nah, beating up on boys bruises their pride too much. I decided to hang back and let them show off to feel good about themselves, you know." I bit my bottom lip bashfully, trying to remember how to flirt as my stomach fluttered.

"Hah! Well, that's awful kind of you. Man, I was sweating bullets as those final points were tallied. How was I going to lose to a girl? One who was a year younger no less.

"I'll tell you what, my number is . . . (couldn't remember one digit, Charlie). I'll be happy to give you a rematch any time to see if your skills have sharpened."

Christian gave me this one-sided, very soft and gentle smile as he drifted backwards to rejoin his friends. I still remember that face floating away because I was so confused by it. I wasn't sure if he was hitting on me or looked at me like a kid sister he could tussle around and give pointers to. I wouldn't have minded a little rough housing in the pool right then and there, if you know what I'm saying.

Christian had a confident kindness and warmth about him. Nothing like Sean's snide, teasing sneer.

I instantly wanted Christian to be my boyfriend, but didn't feel my current crude and crass luring attempts would reel him in. Christian wasn't a trophy to put on the shelf; he was, like, the eye of a tornado where everything on the outside blurred away because nothing else mattered.

In either case, I couldn't tell you one out of ten digits he told to me, and I didn't see him for the rest of the summer. I couldn't forget him though, and my girls wouldn't let me based on the goofy grin and twinkle I got every time they mentioned his name.

Those bitches plastered Margarita and Christian on everything they could find: from notebooks, to soda cups, to bubble gum wrappers. They even got half-way through tattooing it on my arm with permanent marker when we had a sleep over.

How was I supposed to explain "Christian ♥'s" to my mom? I think she got the picture because she softly chuckled over her coffee cup as I spent days trying to scrub that shit off.

February 22, 2010 7:50 PM

When we entered Mason Junior High at the end of summer, I was late and hopelessly lost for my first four classes because as I searched for room numbers, I scanned each and every face in the halls for Christian. It had been almost a month since our fateful first meeting, but my mind had worked me into a frenzy, man.

I mean I regularly dreamed about this kid, Charlie. I thought we were, like, destined to be together. And, if I didn't find him soon, some other swooning damsel might catch his eye. After all, Slimy Sean revealed that boys will only wait so long.

I had all but lost hope by lunchtime and went to drown my sorrows in chocolate milk. (Side note: the best part about junior high was having a choice of chocolate milk. I mean they had skim and 2%, but who would be stupid enough to drink those with fucking chocolate milk available.)

I opened my pink and prissy, cartoon cheerleader lunchbox. I found out later that this was a social foul because all the cool kids' paper bagged their shit, so they wouldn't have to bring it back to their locker, leaving more time to socialize and chill.

I had no appetite because my stomach was filled with the pit of a thought that my lost love was drifting away. I just drooped over the contents of the lunchbox; each item was too heavy to lift to my mouth. I was too sulky to chew.

I think I was about to break down into tears when I was scared out of my skin by the hand that came to rest on my shoulder. "Hey, there you are."

I whirled around like someone was going to hit me and came face to chest with a turquoise and white striped tank-top. I followed the lines to olive skin, a neck, a chin, luscious lips and pearly teeth, and finally those deep ocean eyes. They sparkled just how I remembered, just how I dreamed they would.

"You never called." Christian looked slightly hurt, but his confidence was uncrushable. He wasn't backing down from a challenge, and my completely forgetting his number came off as giving him something to chase.

"No duh, you dip. You, like, rushed through your digits while we were in the water." I shoved his shoulder playfully. "Where was I supposed to write that down, huh?"

"You were supposed to remember. I find myself to be unforgettable." He leaned back, laughing at himself. But, he was only partially kidding. He knew he was hot, so good for him for flaunting it a little.

I jabbed him right back. "Yeah, you're unforgettable alright. You bombarded me in the middle of a crowded pool right after I told off some tool-bag who wanted to date me. And, before you could give me time to remember you from anywhere, you started throwing numbers at me like an Algebra quiz. You're really smooth, you know that?"

Christian rolled his head back and held his belly to laugh. "Maybe those weren't my best moves. Here," Christian took a clicky pen out of his pocket and pulled my left forearm onto his lap. Before I knew what was happening, he'd scrawled "Chris" with "213-555-1011" underneath.

He held out the pen for me to grasp, "Your turn," and put his arm on the table for me to write on. Christian popped up and started to back away. "Make sure to write that down somewhere when you get home. I don't want every girl in school to have my number because you're too afraid to lose it again to wash your arm off."

As he turned down the aisle to leave, he paused. "You coming?" I nearly knocked over my chocolate milk as I scrambled to grab my things. As I obediently followed Christian like a lost puppy, I hugged my unzipped lunch bag a little too tightly to my chest out of the morbid fear I'd dump everything all over the lunchroom floor and be labeled "that girl" for my entire junior high experience.

Christian explained, "My group sits next to the windows because this tool Benny likes to bang the glass when unsuspecting seventh graders pass by for the bathroom.

Benny checks every time one of them comes back to see if he's scared a little piss out of them and shakes the person sitting next to him to point out his successes. He's generally a jerk, but it is kinda funny."

Every conversation stopped when I came to the edge of the table, awkwardly embracing my lunch. Christian put one foot on a stool and leaned over the table to make sure all eyes were on him. "Everybody, this is Margarita." He nodded the back of his head in my direction. When his eyes came back to rest in mine, he waved his hand to the spot next to him. As I gracefully crashed into my seat, Christian made a grand sweeping motion with an outstretched hand, "Margarita, this is everybody," before plopping next to me and chuckling at his own impressive introduction.

February 27, 2010 6:55 PM

I was instantly vaulted into being the queen bee of Mason Junior High. But, this stint as royalty was nothing like before.

I didn't have to lord it over my minions. My old click disappeared because I had entered a higher social class and was terrified that I'd screw it up by associating with the lower class likes of them. I didn't even talk with Brittany and Heather in our pre-algebra class because my prince had whisked me off to his castle and the drawbridge simply wasn't going to lower for them.

Sorry girls.

I completely lost my edge because of how head-over-heals I was for this guy. Chris always sat sideways at the lunch table where his legs would surround me. He wasn't clingy or really touchy. There was just this magnetic heat between us.

For the first time, my mind melted. But, it didn't matter. Chris was the life of the party and would swivel his head like he was watching a Ping-Pong match to keep the conversations rolling. I never got to or had to say much, but I was content, Charlie, wrapped up in Chris's world.

I could tell the groupie girls who hung around were hella jealous of me. They put their time in and then some newbie chick steals the man of all their dreams.

But, they all treated me like the queen. Chris had this infectious, fun, care-free aura about him, and I think the other girls didn't want to lose the chance to bask in that glow even if they couldn't get as close as they wanted to.

Katie was Chris's girl counterpart. She took me right under her wing. Rumor had it that Katie and Chris dated for, like, three days on paper but never went out anywhere or held hands.

The intricacies of young love will always confuse a thoughtful mind.

It was incredible to watch the ebb and flow of the girls and boys and the group. The girls and boys wordlessly knew what days they'd get together, what days they'd remain separate, and which long days would make the two separate groups seamlessly blend at the perfect time.

I swear Chris and Katie secretly got together with, like, their lieutenants and planned it out because that shit was plotted out like a teeny bopper TV show.

March 3, 2010 8:15 PM

Chris and I never really went on any dates, not really. We were always around the larger group of people. But, Chris made sure to drape his long arm around me, and hold my hand, and link our pinkies together at all the right moments.

Most of our together time revolved around before, during, and after school. Mason Junior High had a strict "no macking" policy and physical touch of any kind was strongly discouraged, so young kids wouldn't be led into impregnating each other.

Chris was a badass because he'd skirt the rule by holding my outstretched hand and delicately touching his lips to the end of my fingers. The teachers couldn't bring themselves to address it because Chris was just too fucking smooth, man.

March 9, 2010 7:30 PM

I think part of Chris's charisma came from his parents' house. They had this enormous mansion with the biggest basement I'd ever seen. This was Chris's castle, and his mom and dad kept a never ending supply of pizza, chicken nuggets, burgers, mini corn dogs, and cheese sticks flowing to us any time we were around. Not to mention all the soda we could swallow.

His parents were beautiful people inside and out. They looked like they could model yachts or some shit, being all tanned and toned. The wind would keep Mrs. Jacobson's hair back as Chris's dad would have a powerful hand on her waist with the other hand reaching over her shoulder and securely controlling the wheel of the yacht. They'd look into the great beyond knowing they'd fucking dominate whatever was out there.

Like Chris, his mom and dad knew they were hot shit, but they weren't flashy about it, you know. The love that family had for each other was, like, electric. They never fought or scowled or even paused to skip a beat. They were a regular fifties, black and white TV family.

And, they adored me, Charlie. To this day, I haven't the slightest idea why. But the Jacobson's treated me like I was and would always be their kid.

They invited me over for a couple of family dinners with other aunts and uncles and cousins. They used that mansion to have, like, twenty person family reunions once a month. Mr. Jacobson would be out taming the meat and fire of the grill while Chris's mom would pull perfect dish after perfect dish out of the oven. You could have videotaped it for, like, some morning news cooking show.

Before the feast would start, Mr. Jacobson would ask everyone to bow their heads, and he'd say these beautiful, touching, very personal blessings before we'd dig in.

That's the closest to heaven I think I'll ever get, Charlie. Eating a feast, laughing, and loving those people.

They even brought me to church, and I got to go to a special room where junior high and high schoolers had their own service. I'm pretty sure I knew more about church and God than most of those kids because of Grandpa Bill giving me weekly quizzes. I impressed the minister, Chris, and his family by being able to retell and explain the Bible stories I remembered.

That lovefest of connected and caring people really gave me hope, and for the first time, I cracked the Bible because I wanted to.

I didn't make it all that far because Genesis quickly gets into a bunch of this guy begat that guy who begat these guys. It was like hitting the fast forward button just when the story started getting good.

I did love Jesus there for a while, Charlie. Not really because I had any idea what that meant but because the Jacobson family loved me. Man, I never wanted to leave that place.

March 13, 2010 6:50 PM

While I was weaving my way into a more functional family, Mom was taking every chance she could to get fucked up.

With Uncle Larry around, Mom had a built-in drinking buddy right down the block, and they'd regularly get shitty at the local bars and stumble back to my apartment.

On nights when Mom and Larry planned on whooping it up, it was decided that it would be best for me to crash at Grandma Rosie's for the night. Even though Larry could do no wrong in her eyes, Larry knew better than to stumble into her house drunk as a skunk.

So, I got my old room back, and Larry would rock the couch with Mom at the apartment, and I'd hope to come home without nauseating smells in the air and blotchy carpet marks from where puke had been freshly cleaned.

No matter how well they might have tried, those two fucks just couldn't get it in the toilet. Even when they made it to the bathroom, I'm convinced they missed the fucking bowl with most of it. I'd have to wrap a t-shirt around my nose and mouth to take a wash cloth and cleaning spray to wipe all around and under the toilet just so I could take a piss.

March 19, 2010 7:25 PM

One time, I came home to my mom stumbling around my room struggling to gather my sheets and blankets together. I told her not to worry about cleaning them; that I'd do it. As I scooped up all the sheets with my arms wide and my face buried right in the middle of it all, mom explained that Uncle Larry had brought a lady

81

friend home, and they'd had some fun on my little fucking bed.

I dropped the sheets and began to dry heave. I stripped to my underwear and threw the tainted clothes that had touched my sheets on top of the pile and told my mother, "You've gotta fix this." She said something about making sure to use bleach as I headed for the shower.

The water burned my skin red as I attempted to cleanse myself head to toe three times. No matter how hard I scrubbed, I couldn't wash away the image of Uncle Larry's pasty, ginger, freckled ass rolling around with some bimbo on MY bed.

Mom and I got in a heated argument while I was in my towel because I demanded she scrub the mattress. Her hangover was weighing heavy in her eyes, and I could tell she could barely stand, much less clean. I got dressed and slammed the door on my way to anywhere but there.

I got back after dark, and Mom was passed out, head back and mouth open, slipping sideways down the couch. A big bottle of beer sat mostly empty on the table next to her, and a cigarette was burning a fresh hole in our carpet.

I put the cigarette out and covered her with a blanket. I placed a pillow on the part of the couch where her head would likely land when she slid further, and I ventured into the abyss that used to be my room.

I'd wanted to sleep on the couch that night (and every night after), but good old Mom foiled my plans.

My room reeked of cleanser, which I took to mean that Mom did give my mattress a good scrub. The mattress was still damp, so I flipped it over before redressing my bed with the clean sheets Mom had left in a basket at the bottom of the bed.

From that day forward, I'd strip my bed and hide the good sheets before Mom and Larry would go out. I used a permanent marker to mark the corner of Larry's side and flip it up before leaving. I couldn't stop Larry from bringing home hookers, but at least, I could discourage the floozies from fooling around on my mattress.

March 22, 2010 8:15 PM

When mom got her new gig on the night shift, Saturday nights became a regular shit show. Since Mom was used to sleeping during the day and being up all night, she took advantage of the hours and closed three bars a weekend.

Larry's bum ass worked odd jobs for which he was regularly fired and would rotate excuses to Grandma Rosie about being laid off or the job sight closing. After a couple of rounds of this bullshit, Larry would prep Grandma by saying he was hired on as a temp. That way, when he fucked it up (and he always did), he had a built in excuse.

He jumped the gun too soon and excitedly told everyone that he was being hired on full-time because he became buddies with the business owner's son. Well, the owner shit-canned Larry the next week when he found out Larry had been dealing drugs to his kid and other workers.

I pretty much spent every Saturday night at Grandma Rosie's. I even came up with a pretty good story to explain the situation to the Jacobson's when they had to drop me off at a different house. I told them Mom had picked up an extra shift, so Grandma would be driving me to church on Sunday to let Mom get her rest.

The Jacobson's bought it too because Grandma Rosie would drop me off at their church every Sunday before going to St. Elizabeth's to attend Mass. The Jacobson's would take me out to brunch and pay for my meal, even though I tried to offer them some cash Grandma Rosie gave me. They'd drop me back off at our shitbox apartment in the early afternoon, so Chris and I could "concentrate on our studies."

I always cringed a little as the car stopped, and I was forced back into my sucky reality. I secretly hoped that one day the Jacobson's would just let me stay. Chris and I could have our own separate rooms until we graduated from college, and then, we'd get married and have an apartment of our own and live happy ever after.

That was the dream, Charlie.

Never happened though.

March 27, 2010 7:35 PM

We had a good little routine going until the last hot Saturday night of the season.

Katie had called for a girls' night because Chris and the boys were headed to a shoot 'em up, blow 'em up blockbuster. Personally, I kinda prefer the action packed movies over the mushy gushy kind. I guess that tomboy still lives inside me somewhere.

I wore one of my racy outfits because I would never dare be seen by the Jacobson's in such attire, but I didn't know where I stood with Katie's crew. None of them went to church with us, and they seemed to be into tempting and teasing boys just like the old me used to be.

I already had my prince charming, so I didn't need to put it all out there. But, I wanted to fit in with these girls, and being too goody, goody would only emphasize the fact that I was an underclassman.

Katie put out an enviable spread of nail polish and beauty products. The girls and I got to work manicuring ourselves as the other girls rated and ranked every boy in the eighth grade class.

I only piped up when spoken to, and most of the time, the other girls had to give me detailed descriptions or show me a picture in last year's yearbook for me to offer input.

By the time we got to pairing up to do each other's pedicures, I'd become a fly on the wall. I was happy to just listen and laugh. It felt good to be included without having to put on a show.

Some of the girls revealed their scandalous behavior with this boy or that boy. But, nobody pushed me to divulge. I think they figured I was younger, and they knew Chris was "saving himself," so there were no dirty details to divulge.

At the end of the night, I was lucky to catch a ride with Jennifer's mom. Otherwise, I would have had to hoof it the whole way back to Grandma Rosie's house in this unbearable heat.

I thanked them, and kept the details vague as I ran to the door in the dark.

Grandma was already down for the night, so I turned the key ever so gently and tiptoed my way through the house without any lights.

My room at Grandma Rosie's was upstairs with one of those air conditioners that sits in the window. Uncle Larry had recently pulled it out for the season and plopped it sloppily in the corner. No surprise.

I could feel the temperature rising with each step I took up the stairs.

Despite having opened every window in the upstairs and a fan blasting directly on me, I could not stop sweating.

I stripped down to my bra and thong to get some relief, but sleep was like sloshing back and forth in dewy grass.

I must have fallen asleep at one point because I was shocked awake to see Uncle Larry leaning against my doorway. I'd left my door open to get a breeze from Larry's room which was across the hall from mine. In one hand, Larry held a dripping beer, while he used the other hand to stroke his whipped out dick.

The streetlight outside my window gave off enough light to see his wicked, sickening smirk as he played with himself. I grabbed for the sheets that I'd pushed to the side and covered up.

Larry took a long drag on his beer and placed it on my dresser as he entered the room. His other hand never interrupted its rhythm. "Well aren't you just a little tart. Margarita's got a little Latina ass on her, now doesn't she."

Larry slowly walked to the edge of my bed. "Now, why don't you move those covers and give your Uncle Larry a show, so I can finish up, and we can get some shut-eye?"

I think I thought it was all a nightmare up to that point, but the heavy smell of booze brought me back to my senses, "Get the fuck out, Larry, before I scream! When Grandma finds out what a sick prick you are, she'll have your ass on the next flight back to whatever rock you came from!" I had edged myself all the way into the corner and clutched the covers to my throat as I increased the volume of my threat, "Get OUT!"

Larry used the space I left to put one knee on the bed. His stroke had slowed but never stopped. Larry gave a thoughtful chuckle, "Heh. See that's not how I see this working out little Margarita." Larry's eyes cut to the core of me. They froze me in terror because I could see the emptiness and violence behind them.

Larry lunged and grabbed me by both shoulders. He swiftly flipped me on my stomach and put a knee into my back while grabbing the back of my neck to push my face so hard into the mattress that I could barely breathe.

"Now, don't move," he seethed into my ear.

Larry continued jerking himself off while I was crushed underneath him.

I tried to block it out, but the knee in my back and the hand on my neck bounced in rhythm with his whacking off. I started to vomit as Larry rushed toward the climax, but his load landed at my eye level on the pillow next to me. I held the vomit in to not open my mouth around his jiz.

Larry let out a satisfied exhale and released me.

I rushed back to the corner, trembling under the covers, sniveling and crying. Larry grinned from ear to ear as he tucked his junk back in and zipped his pants . . . slowly . . . casually.

Larry retrieved his beer and took another pull before addressing me. "See, Margarita, if I was you, I'd keep what just happened our little secret. See, you know I'm Rosie's favorite little boy. I can't do no wrong in her eyes. And, you . . . well you is just some little mutt yo momma brought home from the bar one night. Do you know how easy everybody's life would be if they just told you to git?"

Larry let that idea hang for a minute, so it settled in.

"You tell anyone about this, I'll deny it. You push it, and they'll take my side over yours. I been in this family longer. I'm the man of both these houses since your boy Billy kicked it. What are these women gonna do without Ole Larry's help?"

He drained his beer and started to back out the door. Larry stretched out his beer holding hand to point his finger at me, "You'll say nothing if you know what's good for you."

March 30, 2010 6:15 PM

For fuck's sake, Charlie! I know you're a therapist and all, but can't you let this alone? Just for a little while?

You're like a fucking dog with a boner.

Does this shit get you off or something? Like, you picture little, helpless Margarita while you shove your hand down your pants or something?

You sick fuck!

March 30, 2010 9:45 PM

You just don't have any quit in ya, do ya Charlie?

Thought you'd get me good and sauced to loosen my lips.

Well . . . . it worked.

I just fucking hate talking about that night, alright. But, you fucking people: therapists, social workers, counselors, psychiatrists. That's all you fucking want to talk about.

Some people have trouble pinpointing their fucking problem. Half the time, people are so fucking spoiled that they just need to fucking nut-up and enjoy the fucking moment.

Not me.

I know with vivid clarity the moment my life went from kinda charmed to hopelessly fucked up.

Of course I didn't sleep the rest of that night, Charlie! What kind of stupid fucking question is that?

I was stuck, huddled in the corner of that bed shaking. I can't tell whether I was shaking with rage or with fear or both. But, I couldn't fucking move, Charlie.

It seemed like an eternity. I didn't blink once as I watched the door, expecting Larry to come back for seconds.

I don't know what I would have done if he did. What could I do?

When I snapped out of it enough to think a second, I grabbed my clothes and headed for the stairs. I made it to the front door and unlocked and opened it before I realized I was naked and holding my clothes.

My brain fucking failed me, Charlie, because I stood with my hand on the outer door handle debating how far to run down the street and where to hide to put my clothes on.

I was frozen again. I don't know for how long.

Finally, I pulled on my pants and shirt while keeping watch of the bottom of the stairway. I thought I saw the shadows moving which made pulling my clothes on all that much harder.

The shadows followed me all the way down the street.

It wasn't until I turned and locked our apartment door that I felt safe.

But, that didn't last.

I quickly remembered Larry had a key and could come and get me any time he wanted.

I locked myself in my bedroom and pushed a chair into the handle like they do in the movies. I knew it wouldn't hold, but I thought it would at least slow Larry down enough time for me to jump out the window.

I opened the window and pulled the screen out and put it on the floor. I peeked my head out to see how far I'd fall to hit the ground. My window was about a story and a half above the grass. I figured if I dangled and dropped, I'd probably be alright. But then, the possibility of twisting or breaking my ankle gripped me.

Larry would walk slowly as I dragged my leg behind me, desperate to escape. He'd catch me and take me by the hair and drag me to some concrete dungeon and chain my shattered leg to the wall. Larry'd come in at all hours of the day and night to beat me and rape me and cover me in his jiz.

These thoughts swirled as I sat stationed under the window with my arms wrapped around my blanket, shivering,   sweating,   crying.

I must've been aware that the sun was out. But, it didn't move me.

I heard my mom groggily walk her evening's company out. I could hear her rustling about the kitchen making breakfast or coffee or something.

I didn't make a move until Mom came knocking at the door to ask, "Larry? Coffee?"

April 2, 2010 7:15 PM

It took me a couple of minutes to get up. Time seemed to slow down and speed up all at once. Things that I thought were taking forever were happening in a normal amount of time. But then, huge chunks of time would just disappear.

When my body had decided it was safe to move, the first thing I realized is that I was drenched. I mean soaked. At first, I thought it was sweat, but when I stood, I saw a huge shadow marking my carpet. The sharp smell jolted me to the reality that I had pissed myself. And by the looks of it, more than once.

I threw my blanket on the bed, so my mom would think I slept there. I changed out of my dripping clothes and dumped the rest of my dirty laundry out to cover the spot until I could clean it up.

When I emerged, my mom kinda squinted at me, then widened her eyes and squinted again, not believing I was real. "What are you doing here, Rita? I thought you'd be at lunch or something with the boyfriend." She sipped her coffee and returned her attention to the TV.

It was kinda comforting how little Mom gave a shit. When she first looked me over, I thought she'd see right through me to the darkness of that night. I thought she'd be able to smell Larry's boozy breath, or his sweat, or his sex stain like I could. But for her, the events of last night just meant another hung over Sunday.

I recited the lie I'd practiced in my bedroom, "Grandma's house was hot as hell, so I snuck home to sleep in my bed."

"Huh," she said sipping her coffee and remaining mesmerized by the TV. "Where's Larry then?"

Just the mention of his name made me panic. My pulse was throbbing in my neck and pounding in my ears. Whatever I said next would surely give me away. "I didn't see him when I got in." It was the truth.

"Ha!" Mom smirked and shared, "He probably got so shitty, he forgot where he slept. He was chatting up that blond with the huge knockers. I thought she had more self-respect; but good for Larry."

Never once did Mom look back at me. I think my eyes would have pleaded with her to ask me more questions until I confessed.

Instead, I scurried back to my room and passed out on my unmade, Larry-side-up bed.

A knock startled me out of my blackout. "What?!?" I asked all groggily and bitchy.

"It's six o'clock, Rita. I thought you'd be hungry," my mom answered, sounding a little bit concerned.

"Oh, yeah. I must've dozed off." I wiped the drool and tried to rub life back into the side of my face that had been plastered to the mattress.

I was pulling my hair back as I opened the door, and Mom was standing right there, "Are you okay, hun?"

The surprise of her standing in my doorway launched me backwards, tripping over the corner of the bed and twisting to sprawl across the floor. I must've looked horrified because my mom rushed in to kneel at my side.

I had to force myself to smile; to pretend I wasn't broken, "Yeah Ma, I'm fine. Or, at least, I was until you scared me half to death."

She put her palm on my forehead still concerned. "You feel a little warm, Rita. Do you feel sick?"

Mom gave me an out and an easy explanation for all the recent strangeness, so I thought I'd take it. "Yeah. I have been feeling a little dizzy. I think I got too much heat."

"That's what I told Christian." *Christian! Oh shit!* My mom reminded me I'd stood Christian and his family up for church with zero explanation. "He left a message before we woke up, and he called back about half an hour ago. He seemed worried because you never called. I told him you'd been sleeping and were probably sick."

"Thanks, Ma. I'll call him," I brushed passed her to hide the fear I knew was growing in my eyes.

"Don't screw it up, Rita," Mom advised me. "Good men are hard to find. Trust me; I know. That Christian is such a nice boy and comes from a great family. And, they have money. You might not be thinking about that, but let me tell you, it doesn't hurt." Mom chuckled and winked at me, and I couldn't help but bashfully grin back.

I did love Chris. And, I think he loved me too.

April 5, 2010 7:30 PM

The guilt hit me like a sledgehammer after dinner that night. I went to my room to call Chris, but I couldn't bring myself to dial. I picked up the phone and put it down. I started to dial and hung up. I even got as far as one ring before slamming it down and cursing myself for being such a coward.

But, a man had violated me, Charlie. How was I supposed to tell Chris that? How could I? Should I even tell Chris what had happened? Would Chris still want damaged goods? Will Chris think I invited or enticed Larry's actions? I mean, I was in my bra and panties. Will Chris believe I said no and resisted?

Will it even matter?

Chris was saving himself for me or whoever he married. And now, I was tarnished,   used,   defiled.

I didn't talk to Chris until school the next morning when he came rushing up behind me at my locker, "What happened to you yesterday?" Chris tried to hide behind a flirty smirk, but his eyes shifted between concern and anger.

"I'm soooo sorry, Chris," I whined pathetically. "I was supposed to sleep over at my grandma's, but her place was super hot, and I ended up wandering home, deliriously, in the middle of the night and slept until like noon." I kept my light hoody perched on my head to help avoid eye contact and began to head to class. My fashion choice doubled as support for my cover story of being sick.

Before I turned the corner, Chris grabbed at my arm at the elbow and let his fingers slide down as I walked away to the desperate, pleading edge of my fingertips. "Do you still love me?" he begged with big puppy dog eyes.

God, that guy was fucking smooth, Charlie.

Here I was wrestling with my own unworthiness, and Chris was losing sleep thinking I was going to break up with him or something. "Of course I do. I'm just not myself, and I don't want to get you sick, silly."

Chris bowed as he pulled my dangling fingers to his lips, "The price we pay for love."

April 8, 2010 8:15PM

During that week, I started to regain the ability to sleep. I think I told myself that it was a one-time thing. Larry wasn't going to barge into my apartment to come get me. Larry was drunk and horny and got turned down by some bimbo. He didn't know what he was doing. He's probably too ashamed to apologize.

We won't talk about it.

It WON'T happen again.

I started to believe the lie, too, Charlie.

Larry called in sick to the following weekend's drunk-fest, and I convinced Mom to let me stay home and sleep in my own bed. After all, I was almost thirteen and did it every school night anyway.

Mom didn't argue much. She couldn't admit that she didn't want me there because the possibility of me hearing her moaning while grinding some random dude's dick might ruin the mood for her. I'm sure she made a deal with herself that she could keep her bedroom antics somewhat low-key for just one night.

She didn't end up brining anyone home that night anyway.

Things with Chris started to go back to normal, too. I went back to adoring being gently guided by the tips of my fingers to wherever Christian decided to lead us.

No one was going to bring up what happened. I certainly didn't want to admit it. Larry definitely wouldn't tell.

At some point, the experience faded into memory like a bad dream.

The only leftover of that fucked up night was a gnawing feeling that Christian didn't find me physically desirable. I know he'd never have cheated on me, and I know we were supposed to be saving our virginity for marriage and shit. But, I felt like he should be struggling a little more to keep his hands off me.

The heat that lived in the spaces between us had cooled for me. I'd tried to spark it again by closing the gap.

I needed to be touching Chris at all times. It started with just gently, barely brushing him. Arm on arm, legs touching, feet touching. I just needed to be closer. To feel secure. To feel loved.

I started laying my head like a puppy on his shoulder. I'd pull his hand to rub my cheek and then kiss it. I realize now how desperate I was for Chris to get lost in my eyes and forget everything else around us.

I wanted to be the center of his universe.

I realized then that our sparse kisses had only been affectionate pecks that you'd give a sister or your mom. I wanted Chris to grab me and kiss me deeply. I wanted our faces to smash together and for us to try to swallow each other. I wanted us to lose control, if only for a moment. And, I wanted to feel the rush of reality and regret that we almost . . .

But, he never did.

April 12, 2010 6:45 PM

It took a month, but Larry got me again.

It seemed like everything had gone back to normal. Grandma and Mom even took me out for our fall mall shopping trip. My fashion had become considerably more covered up. Somewhat because I was dating Christian and hanging out at church, but I think not wanting to have Larry and other unwanted people staring at me was a big part as well.

When I was younger and teasing and tantalizing boys, I don't think I ever really realized what it might lead to.

Now, I just wanted to be able to cover up and hide. If I could have pulled my hood down over my face and disappear, life would've been so much better.

I even went back to spending Saturdays at Grandma Rosie's during Mom and Larry's benders. I think it was the third or fourth weekend when it happened again.

I'd sleep with the door locked at Grandma's. The first two weeks I even shoved a chair under the handle to prevent entry.

I could barely sleep, and when I did, I woke up, like, once an hour from the nightmares.

I was terrified of leaving the fortress that was my room to pee. I had just woken up from Larry pinning me down and tearing off my clothes, and I'd had to pee, bad. I stared at the blocked door; sure that Larry would barge through at any moment.

My first bathroom attempt was a no go, Charlie. I went to the door and shuttered. It took forever to take enough deep breaths just to move the fucking chair.

I got stuck on the lock. If I turned the lock, Larry could rush in, and then, I was a goner. The closer I got to unlocking the door, the more my hand shook. I couldn't grip it, Charlie. My hand wouldn't open the door.

Enough time had passed that I had dribbled in my panties a little. My attention was drawn away from the door and Lurking Larry in the hallway. My brain was drawn to my burning bladder, and I sure as hell wasn't going to piss myself again because of Larry.

I tipped over the garbage can to dump out its contents in the corner. I quietly promised Grandma Rosie that I'd clean up the mess tomorrow as I squatted over the plastic can.

I don't know if Larry had tried to come in those other nights or not. But, I fucked myself by forgetting to block the door with the chair that third night.

I don't know if that would have stopped him, and I guess we'll never find out.

The smell of beer in the air drew me out of my sleep. At first, Larry standing in the doorway with a dripping beer bottle seemed like another nightmare. He sipped his beer and smiled his creepy smile, "Ello there, Margarita. Ole Uncle Larry struck out at the pub tonight. I thought

I'd had something going, but this whore stiffed me after I bought her three rounds. The Bitch!"

I glanced over to see where I'd left the chair. It couldn't help me now.

Nothing could.

"Anyway, Love. She left me with this throbbing cock, and I just can't seem to fall asleep when I've got these blue balls here."

I backed myself into the corner. I kept trying to push back with my feet on the bed and my knees to my chest. I pushed my back as far into the wedge of the corner as I could. When I had squished myself as far away from Larry as I could be in that tiny room, I hoped to melt through the wall, become a part of the wall, even bust through the wall and fall to the ground. Anything to keep Larry from touching me.

"Now, don't be like that, Rita. I just need a bit of a boost to get me there. Why don't you drop your drawers and give Larry a looksee at that tight little Latina ass you got working there?"

I didn't budge. I couldn't. I think I knew if I just showed Larry some skin, he'd do his business and leave. But, I couldn't move. I was frozen. Terrified.

"Last chance, Rita. Before we have to do this the hard way."

Larry stared at me with hungry, starving, violent eyes. He took a long pull on the beer before setting it down.

His eyes seemed to register a deep longing pleasure as he climbed across the bed and grabbed me.

Larry flipped me on my stomach again and pulled my pants down to expose my ass. But, he didn't hold me down this time.

"Now, just sit still, Little Rita. This'll be over quick."

I was still too scared to move. But despite the throbbing terror in my ears, I could still hear Larry unzip his pants. He exhaled, deep and long, as he began to stroke it. I heard my pulse and shoved my face deeper into the pillow afraid I'd let out a scream.

But, I was helpless.

I heard Larry's steady scraping of flesh on flesh. I heard his labored breathing. I could tell he was struggling.

Fucking Larry was too fucking drunk to get it up, but he found motivation to fucking molest me!

That's just shitty, Charlie.

I don't know when Larry finished up. I got lost somewhere in his rhythm or my terror and rage. And then, he was just . . . . . gone.

This time, I wasted no time. I pulled up my pants and got the fuck outta there.

I hoofed it down the stairs and out the door and sprinted as far away from that house as fast as I could.

About halfway between Grandma's and our apartment, I slowed down thinking that the cops would stop and question a lunatic running at four in the morning, and I wouldn't know what to say.

I walked fast. It didn't last. I saw a shadow, and I busted my ass back to my apartment thinking, F*uck the police!*

I locked our door and locked my room and backed into the window and collapsed. I kept pushing backwards. My feet sliding on the carpet. My back pressing against the wall.

Until I gave up.

My head fell between my knees. I shook, and I sobbed.

I wanted for it to end.

I wanted, more than anything, just to die in that moment, Charlie.

And, my feet kept trying to push me back; away from it all.

April 13, 2010 7:15 AM

Man, Doc . . . Charlie . . . Whatever . . . There's something to this getting shit off your chest thing.

I've never told any single person all the gritty details about what happened to me. I think I thought that part of it was my fault, and I was already in trouble, so the last thing I wanted was to dig any deeper.

But fuck, Charlie. I slept like a baby last night.

I don't think I fell asleep so much as I passed the fuck out. When I woke up, it felt like my soul was raising up to reenter my body. I woke up confused as hell. I didn't know where I was or what day it was or what time it was. Hell Chuck, I didn't even know who I was.

For the first time in a long, long ass time, I woke up happy. I don't know what it is. Staying here? Talking with you? I feel lighter. I feel like there are possibilities that I never thought I'd have again.

I can feel hope.

Just a little, Charlie. But, it's there. Down deep; it's there.

I think I'm gonna take your advice, Charlie, ole boy. I think I'll look into that GED thingy.

There might just be a future for Margarita yet.

April 17, 2010 7:50 PM

For a while there, Charlie, I thought I had gotten one step ahead of Uncle Larry. This shit happening twice was no accident; I knew that. Larry would and could come and get me and use me whenever the fuck he felt like it.

Up to that point, there was nothing physical about his attacks. He didn't touch me. He didn't ask me to touch him.

But, the fucking nightmares. They were vivid as shit, Charlie. They felt real.

I'd wake up somewhere between Larry tearing off my clothes, and Larry forcing himself inside me. When I'd wake, I could still feel the pressure in the pit of my stomach; the pain of being raped.

I got used to slapping my hands over my mouth to muffle the screams that would come. I'd shake and sweat and cry all huddled up and pathetic until the darkness would take me again.

I couldn't help it, Charlie. I'd tell myself it wasn't real.

But, it felt real.

The fear was real.

The pain was real.

April 20, 2010 6:45 PM

Despite molesting me, Larry was still family.

Thanksgiving was torture. Sitting at a tiny table across from Larry, I couldn't force myself to eat a bite. I wanted to. I even tried a couple of times because Grandma's food smelled so good, and my stomach was turning in knots. But, every time the food would hit the back of my throat, I'd gag. It even made me have a coughing fit at one point that drew everyone's attention during that quiet, tense meal.

Mom and Grandma still didn't really get along. They were peaceful because they both had to care for me. But, the longer they were around each other, the edgier they got.

Grandma didn't really drink. But, the holidays brought out the best in her. I caught her sipping the cooking wine, and she'd overfill her glass during dinner and never let it dip below half full.

Mom and Larry used the festivities as an excuse to get shitty in front of Grandma. God knows she was in no shape to keep track of them or lecture anyone.

After dinner that Thanksgiving was the first time I got good and tipsy. I was cleaning the plates next to several open bottles of wine. I snuck some pours from each bottle into my water bottle. The water bottle wasn't clear, and it was closable, so I thought the smell wouldn't get out. Plus, I was a goody goody, so anyone who thought they'd smelled something probably would blame it on their own breath.

The icing on the night was all the drunks having a few laughs at a family, holiday comedy. In my stupor, I passed out on Grandma Rosie's shoulder.

It was the first time in a long time that I had a good night sleep. I slept all the way through until morning and woke up in my room at Grandma's house.

When I came down for breakfast, Grandma explained that Larry was nice enough to carry me from the couch up to my room.

April 24, 2010 8:10 PM

I got drunk on Thanksgiving for the same reason everyone else did; it was just too fucking hard to sit around that table and not acknowledge how fucked up we all were.

Mom and Larry were a hot fucking mess; always waiting for their next, temporary fix. Grandma was a puddle without Grandpa Bill. She was a great second banana, but she couldn't lead this bunch.

I was broken into a million little pieces, Charlie. And, nobody at that table was gonna help fix me.

Grandma Rosie had asked us to share what we were thankful for. This was a tradition that Grandpa Bill had taken very seriously because he wanted us to notice and appreciate all the little blessings we had in life. He'd told me that it's the little things that get us through the toughest times.

Everybody half-assed it without Grandpa Bill to make it meaningful. I think I said some bullshit about being in a new school and learning a lot.

I had to hide my tears because talking about school reminded me that Christian had broken up with me a week before my birthday. He said some bullshit about how he loved me, but we weren't meant to be and that God had a plan for both of us.

I had had some cracks in my life, Charlie. But, that brought the whole fucking thing crumbling down.

Where was I supposed to find a group of friends? Everyone I ate lunch with in junior high was a year older than me, and all of them were friends with Christian. I couldn't go back to that table.

I had sold my previous click out in order to date Chris. And, I'm sure they weren't gonna just forgive and forget and let me be their queen again. Brittany had gotten some backbone and taken over when I left. She wasn't gonna give it up without a fight.

Who was I supposed to lean on to get through this tough shit? I'd banked on that Christian and I having this forever type of love. I was part of his family. I'd even sold my family out to get more of his. Not like my mom minded not having to keep track of me. She'd always said she wanted a better life for me, and I think she knew the Jacobson's were giving it to me.

At least, for a little while.

The worst part of the whole thing, Charlie, was losing my church. I'd never felt such a sense of belonging before. I was part of something. I had a big ass group of people who, like, legit loved me. I haven't been able to find that ever since.

I was an extension of the Jacobson's at Christ Church. And without them, I wasn't sure I'd be welcome. At best, I'd be pitied like a prodigal child. Someone who was lost and without a home.

I didn't want people who saw me as part of the group one day to see me as trying to peak in from the outside the next.

The youth pastor, Jaime, called me once when I didn't show up for a couple weeks. I didn't call him back, and my connection to Christ Church unraveled as quickly as it had started.

April 28, 2010 7:15 PM

I got used to being alone pretty quick. I kinda liked it. I even made a game out of avoiding situations and places that made me uncomfortable.

I'd rush in and out of the lunchroom, eating and then heading to the library. The crowds and the noise that used to get me excited and, like, give me energy now made me fucking paranoid, Charlie.

I thought every laugh was a joke made about me. I tried to hear every whisper, and then, I'd jump when a group would laugh loudly. That tool Benny even made me piss myself because he'd pounded the glass inches from my face when I walked past.

We were friends like a week ago, bitch! You can't give me a break?

I never realized how cruel that shit was until I was on the receiving end. Benny really is a stupid fucking jackass!

The school librarian became my new buddy. She wouldn't bother me when I fell asleep in a cubicle. I think she knew I needed it.

With Uncle Larry chasing me almost every night in my dreams, I was a mess, Charlie. My grades fell like a stone in the ocean. I went from mostly A's and a couple B's to mostly D's with an occasional C.

I'd used the parent-teacher conferences to get permission to go to the library during lunch to "study more." It was hard to watch the pained expression on Mom and my teacher's faces as they tried to figure out how I tanked an entire semester so quickly. They blamed the breakup and a broken heart, which was a part of it, no doubt. But, if they had known the truth, if they could feel my pain, even only second hand, I think their wincing faces would have broken and shattered.

Just like me.

May 2, 2010 7:35 PM

At some point, I just skipped out on the lunchroom. There was no eating in the library. No exceptions! But, I huddled in a back corner, and Ms. Swanson gave me the space I desperately needed.

She always had a warm greeting for me that made me feel unjudged and accepted. I'm sure she knew I was broken. Unlike other people, Ms. Swanson never tried to fix me. I think she realized that some wounds take time to callous over. They're not gonna heal right anyway and picking at them is only going to make it worse.

Ms. Swanson's library was like a bandage. It protected me while my wounds tried to close.

I don't know how much it helped. But, it definitely didn't hurt.

I think Ms. Swanson gave me a chance to escape my fucked up life, if only for a couple minutes. She was a nasty bitch to most of the other students. Probably because the other kids were fucking clowns, and Ms. Swanson had to babysit entire classes while the teachers stepped out for a smoke break.

I don't think I ever really thanked her. If I get the chance to swing by Mason Junior High, I think I'll look her up. She should know how much she helped me, how protected I felt all those periods in her library.

May 5, 2010 8:40 PM

My hiding from the world wasn't as obvious as the game of cat and mouse I played with Larry. When I would stay at Grandma's, I'd set an alarm for one a.m. I couldn't sleep much anyway, but I wanted to be up and dressed and waiting by the back door in case Larry'd come stumbling in.

The first couple of times, I fell asleep huddled in my coat and sweating my ass off. When the sun would peak out, I'd run back upstairs, so Grandma wouldn't catch me. Grandma Rosie didn't think twice about a teenager sleeping in so late.

A couple of nights, I got the best of Larry. He'd open the front door all sloppy and loud, and I'd sneak out the back. I'd come around the side of the house and make sure Larry was inside before bolting down the block towards our apartment.

Even drunk as a skunk, Larry figured out my plan after a couple tries. Larry came home and fiddled with the door to get me to run outside. When I came around the house, I ran headfirst into Larry's chest.

He grabbed me before I could scream and covered my mouth and lifted and dragged me to the garage in the backyard. Larry had to let go of my mouth to get the keys to open the garage. But before he did, he whispered in to my ear, "Don't scream, Margarita. How will you explain being outside in your coat at this hour?" His breath suffocated me with the smell of beer and vomit. I couldn't breathe; I couldn't think; and I was trying to hold back my own gagging cough.

Larry was right. How could I explain this?

Larry shoved me into the dusty garage and shut the door behind us. A single, hazy bulb gave outlines to the shapes in the garage. As the bulb heated up, things became more clear, including all the floating dust we'd kicked up as we shuffled in.

"Drop them drawers, Margarita." Larry licked his lips like a wolf that was about to lunge and devour me.

My mind was frozen. I couldn't think of any way to get out. Larry was too strong and had the door and the garage opener blocked. I could have tried to jump in my

Grandma's car to open the garage door. But, the possibility of being stuck in a tight space while Larry grabbed and groped to pull me out was a terrifying thought straight from my nightmares.

I turned around to give Larry what he was looking for.

"All the way down, Rita." Larry instructed me how to best help get him off. "Lift up your jacket for me, will ya, darling?"

I squeezed my eyes shut to prevent the tears from coming. I wanted to believe if I closed them hard enough and long enough, when I opened them, none of this would have actually happened.

My hands balled around and wrung my jacket like I'd like to have choked Larry.

I don't know if it was my arms getting tired from being so tense or the shiver caused by my ass freezing, but I began to sway uncontrollably. I didn't even bother trying to stay still. I figured a little dance might help Larry get off quicker.

"Turn around, Rita."

The request shocked me back to the moment. My eyes popped open to take in a foggy, hazy garage. My panting breath created mist in the air that blocked me from being able grasp what was going on. I looked backwards over my shoulder see my uncle panting and shaking with a devilish smirk on his face.

"I said, 'Turn around, Rita.'"

I desperately wanted nothing more than to squeeze my eyes shut to escape this place this moment. But, I thought, *this is it*. My nightmares had come true, and Larry was about to stab me with his dick right here on the cold, concrete floor.

As I turned, I couldn't help but follow Larry's pathetic convulsions to his pulled-out cock.

"Wanna touch it, Rita?"

My immediate gag gave Larry the message that he'd have to continue on his own.

I tried again to shut my eyes tight enough escape this place, but Larry's hand stroking a cock that looked like it wanted to lunge and plunge into me prevented me from keeping them closed.

I looked at Larry's slob face as he drooled over my naked pussy. I stared into the rafters, looking over every inch of the ceiling for a way to escape.

Larry's groans brought my vision back down to see his load splash at my feet.

I jumped back and quickly pulled up my pants. "Run along, Rita," he gasped.

Uncle Larry had the most satisfied grin, beaming with spit dangling from his chin.

"Go on, now. Run along."

May 10, 2010 6:55 PM

I outfoxed Larry the next time he tried to get me. When I heard him jangling his keys in the front door, I snuck out back and ducked out the gate to the back alley.

It was pitch fucking black, Charlie. That's why I didn't go that way to begin with. My mind could only imagine what kind of monsters lurked down that narrow alley.

But, I definitely knew what kind of monster was waiting if I went back.

So, I ran toward the street, guided by the light in the distance.

May 13, 2010 10:40 PM

I've seen the way you've been looking at me, big boy. My stories are starting to hurt you, aren't they? You want to know if Margarita has been taken and tainted by Uncle Larry, don'tcha?

I thought you didn't care about my past, Charlie? I thought we both "had baggage?" But, I caught you, good doctor.

During my first couple of stories, I thought you were getting your rocks off on this shit. But lately, I've noticed that you weren't really liking the picture of little, vulnerable Margarita being abused.

I can guess the conclusion that you've probably jumped to. You think he raped me. You think Uncle Larry had his way with Little Maggie.

The truth is I've been trying to figure out if that would turn you off or on. Do you have that Big Daddy fantasy where you spank the little girl?

You can spank me, Charlie. I might even like it.

And no, Charlie. Larry didn't fuck me. He never had the chance.

May 17, 2010 7:10 PM

My back alley escape was quickly blocked by Horny Larry.

I was all dressed and ready to run, slumped next to the backdoor.

To make a quick escape, I had unlocked the door and even had it popped a little, so I wouldn't have to turn the nob.

I never thought that Larry could take advantage of this just as easily as I could.

Luckily, I was sitting close enough for the inside door to hit my leg when Larry tried to get the jump on me. I was in the middle of a nightmare where Larry had his hands pressed to my shoulders, pinning me, paralyzing me. The real bump from the door jarred both worlds together, and I let out a screech that woke me right the fuck up.

Larry shoved the door into me and yanked me to my feet before covering my mouth.

He was too late.

"Who's there? Maggie? Is that you?" Grandma must have been as startled by the scream as I was, "Are you alright?"

Grandma emerged to find me and Larry standing in the open doorway with our winter coats on in the middle of the night, "What in the blue blazes is going on?"

Grandma must've been completely lost at the sight. I didn't know what to say because I was sneaking around her house when I was supposed to be upstairs sleeping.

Slick Larry helped us all out. "Sorry, Ma. I was trying to come in quietly, and I bumped into Maggie in the hallway."

Grandma was even more confused. "I thought you were going to stay at Angela's tonight. That's why Maggie is sleeping over."

"I was, Ma," Larry twitched is search of an answer. "But, Angie has company over, so I thought I'd just sleep in my own bed."

The silence felt like an eternity as Grandma groggily tried to put this all together. "Maggie, what are you doing all dressed up for the cold."

I was too caught up watching Larry fumbling through his story to make up one of my own. I panicked and mumbled, trying to piece the right lie together.

Larry bought me time by moving to Grandma's side in the hallway, "Yeah Maggie, what are you doing up so late?"

That prick fucking dared me to tell my Grandmother in front of him that he was molesting me regularly. He dared me to tell her that I couldn't sleep because I was terrified that my sleazy uncle would get me whether I was awake or dreaming.

"I couldn't sleep. I, I, I . . . I just wanted to sleep in my own bed in my own room."

"Oh, you poor dear." Grandma put a supportive hand on my cheek. "You just run along up to bed, and I'll get you home after breakfast."

Grandma turned back to her room. Though she was older than God, her word was final.

Larry waved his hand as if to say, *after you*. And, I ran ahead of him to my room.

I locked the door and pushed the chair under the handle and sat in the corner of my bed with my coat and shoes still on, watching for the knob to turn.

Larry made no attempt to get in that night.

He did wish me a goodnight, "This isn't over, Margarita." And, I could hear his fingers scraping down the door as he left.

May 21, 2010 8:15 PM

There was a long stretch there where Larry left me alone. I think Grandma had spooked him.

Larry could beat up, abuse, and intimidate me, but he had a soft spot for Grandma. She'd always taken care of him. And, I think Larry was staying there partially to return the favor.

I still would spend most Saturdays at Grandma's. I'd make sure to lock and block the door every time I tried to sleep. The nightmares would haunt me whether I was asleep or awake because Larry lived in the dark parts of my mind. I regularly peed in the garbage can because it made me feel safe and in control.

And Larry, . . . well I don't really know if he ever tried to get in.

Several mornings when I moved the chair, I found the door unlocked. I was sure I'd locked it.

It scared the living shit out of me, Charlie. Was Larry unlocking the door to just fuck with me?

Or, was he trying to get in and blocked by the chair?

Did he not push through because he didn't want to wake up Grandma again?

Why didn't I wake up?

These thoughts raced through my mind every time I'd lay my head on the pillow. They made it so the nightmares never quite stopped or ever really slowed down.

May 25, 2010 7:25 PM

A couple months after Christian had dumped me, I got some pity from this girl Gina who grew up a couple houses down from the Jacobson's.

She was like this punk-rock princess. She was beautiful. I think prettier than me or any of the other girls that hung in the Christian click. But, she hid it behind a lot of baggy black clothing, jet black hair, and dark make-up. Black rings both hid and drew people into her eyes in most mesmerizing way. Electric red lipstick and nails made her pail skin look white as snow.

Gina gave me a couple of weeks to recover before she asked about Christian kicking me to the curb. I think she saw how quick my social rise turned into a colossal crash and burn.

Unlike the other eighth grade girls I'd met who were mostly worried about their own social standing, Gina didn't give a FUCK. She was gonna do what she wanted to do when she wanted to do it and would bitch out anyone who got in her way.

My previous personality required an all eyes on me approach, much like other girls. As I tried to find a new life in hiding, I really grew to appreciate what Gina had going on.

She could cut through the hallways of the school like a hooded phantom; unbothered and unnoticed. If she wanted to commit a crime, no one could identify her because she had this ability to melt into the background.

When she chose to socialize, she took over our group. Even Katie was scared to put her in her place because Gina so fiercely bucked the order of things. Being loud and edgy, she'd capture the boys' attention and the girls' jealousy at the same time because she was fearless.

She was free.

Gina and Chris grew up a couple houses away from each other and hung out since they were, like, in diapers. Christian said Gina went all Goth and shit at some point in seventh grade. Christian could never figure out why. But, being the good Jesus Freak that he is, Chris continued to invite her to church stuff when he saw her on the bus.

Gina would show up occasionally. Half the time, she'd come and go without anybody even noticing her. The other times she was the life of the party.

I desperately wanted to catch some of her confidence.

I think Gina caught me staring at her in the cafeteria one day while shoveling down my food. I was trying to figure out how to disappear, and I got caught in the act right off the bat.

"Don't tell me you're switching sides after Christian dumped you?" Gina made me jump out of my skin. In my cubicle hideaway, I wasn't used to hearing anything but my thoughts. "I mean, I'm flattered, but I'm not planning on going through my lesbian phase until college. If you can stick it out until then, we can see where this goes."

When I caught my breath enough to ask, "How did you get in here?"

Gina produced a crumpled, red hall pass. "That's not the right date," I noticed.

"Yeah, I've been using this for a solid six weeks. I think that's a new record." Gina explained that the writing on any pass is too small to read on the fly. "The key is shoving it close enough to somebody, so they could have read it but removing it before they actually can. Most people won't ask to see it again because they're embarrassed that they weren't paying attention. This one doesn't even have my name on it." Gina showed me the name of Dominic Spaner who neither one of us had heard of.

May 30, 2010 8:00 PM

Gina's risky reintroduction created a sisters-in-the-hoods bond that guided me into a new life.

Hanging out with Gina was like being by myself with somebody else. We'd mainly watch videos, eat junk food, and wander around. Sometimes we'd be looking for people. Other times we'd be looking to hide. Most times, we'd be pulling epic pranks.

Gina had this hilariously gross way of sticking her chewed gum to the bottom of a doorknob.

We'd try to remain inconspicuous by sitting casually against a locker or hiding around a corner to watch. Each person who would grab the door would jump back and check their hand. Then, they'd bend down low and search around the doorknob. About half the people would use, like, two fingers to turn the knob over and discover the gum. The others would bend and twist or sit on the ground to find what we left them.

We'd usually scurry away trying to hold in our laughs. A science teacher, Mr. Felding, caught us because a particularly goofy Gina let out a squeal too soon. His chubby ass couldn't keep up with us, but he did know Gina from class, so she got called down to the office later.

She said that she didn't get in trouble because they couldn't prove shit. But, we decided to cool off to let the attention die down.

Charlie, can you believe how fucked up people are?

We didn't lose a lot of our gum supply because most people we pranked just squeezed the top of the door handle to get through and left the gum. We'd get multiple people with the same piece.

Our record was twelve fucking people with one stick of gum. That's just messed up, Charlie.

June 3, 2010 6:45 PM

Our other prank involved ketchup packets in the bathroom. We'd go together and place four ketchup packets under the seat where the nubs touch the bowl. The idea was when some bitch would sit down, the packets would explode into her pussy, her ass, and pretty much everywhere else. If we were lucky, some would hit a bitch's pants the right way and look like their period leaked.

We didn't have to wait outside the bathroom long to hear the squeals and screams. Girls took forever to come out, trying to clean that shit as best they could before emerging. Some girls tried to tie a sweater around their waste to hide it. Others had noticeable wet-spots where they had to blot that shit out.

I would have chosen water over a red smear too.

The game lost its luster a little when some nerdy chick named Jezebel came out crying and ran straight to the office. Her mom had to come pick her up and BITCHED THE PRINCIPAL OUT!!!

After that, signs were posted in each stall to leave the seats up after every use. The cafeteria even switched to using big bowls of ketchup with spoons.

I don't know that we would have continued anyway. The point of the game was to get the popular girls and the wannabes. You know, the prissy bitches with some rod stuck up their stuffy butts.

This girl wasn't like that. She came to school for school. She didn't bother anybody. She barely spoke at all.

In the brutal jungle of middle school girls, we made that girl's life even harder than it already was.

That shit really affected me, Charley. I'd temper down Gina's pranks when I thought they'd hurt like that. If Gina was gonna do what she did anyway, I'd peace-out for a little while because I didn't want anybody to feel how I felt when I sprinkled my pants because that asshole Benny spooked me.

That shit scars, Charley.

I'm mean, I'm like totally beyond it. But, thinking about it gets me a little teary.

I still feel bad for Jezebel. I hope she blooms from a nerd into, like, a beauty queen and runs circles around these other bitches with her brains, too.

I really do.

June 6, 2010 7:15 PM

I never thought my mom getting locked up would be such a blessing, but it really was, Charlie.

My mom was on a bender one Friday night with Larry, and Larry's dumb ass decides to try to pick a fight. Nothing really happened, and the bouncers separated them, but when the cops got there, Larry was wasted, and they decided to arrest him to let him sleep it off or something.

My mom, being the big sister that she was and being skunk-drunk herself, didn't like the police putting handcuffs on Uncle Larry. She got pushy with the cops, trying to break Larry free, and when the cops moved her back, she slapped one across the face.

The cop tried to arrest her, but she struggled and ended up donkey kicking this guy right in the balls. Larry wasn't in the squad car yet, so the other cop couldn't chase my mom. She ran for it with handcuffs on one arm.

She didn't have much time to panic because the bouncer told the cops who she was, and she got picked up, like, minutes after making it home.

Grandpa Bill left Grandma Rosie enough money to live on, but she definitely didn't have the ten grand sitting around to bail my mom out.

I got a rest from leering Larry because Grandma assigned him to take care of my mom's apartment, and I was gonna move back in with Grandma. Larry didn't put up much of a fight because Grandma did post the five hundred bucks to get his ass outta the slammer.

I think he figured a little time and distance would help Grandma forget what a dipshit he is.

June 8, 2010 6:20 PM

I actually started enjoying life again with Gina around. Doing a complete one-eighty from being the queen bee of the sixth grade to a goody-goody church girl to a punk rock all-star was freeing, Charlie.

When I was with Christian and even before that, my life revolved around what people thought of me. With Gina, we didn't give a shit and even went out of our way to fuck with people. I think we figured if people were gonna hate on us, might as well give them a reason.

Gina was like me, and she hooked an eighth grader when she first made it into middle school.

Jordan Knox was the baddest of the bad. Evidently, he got in so many fights when he was at Mason that they threatened to expel him. His mom definitely couldn't control him, so he had to go live in South Carolina on a military base with his dad.

It didn't take long for his dad to whip him into shape. As Jordan tells it, his dad put him through basic training and shit.

Dad would set an alarm to wake Jordan up at, like, four A.M. If Jordan wasn't dressed and out of his room in five minutes, his dad would flip his bed, dump water on him, or rub frozen peas on Jordan's chest. Then, his dad would bark and play sirens at Jordan through a megaphone and chase Jordan on a five mile run.

Jordan said he puked the whole first week. Towards the end of a run, when he didn't have any food left to chuck, Jordan would dry heave and turn purple and not breathe and shit. Once, Jordan even blacked out. His dad shook him awake and, like, lifted him up to get him to keep running before he could even see anything again.

Gina was heartbroken when Jordan was shipped off. This was just before I met her, and I think Jordan being gone caused her to give the Christian click a second try. Maybe being around the normal crew was too tough without Jordan around.

Middle school love isn't forever, and a couple of weeks after Jordan broke off their long-distance love affair, Gina moved onto a goon named Marco. I mean you couldn't find two more opposite people.

Gina was skinny as a pole, and Marco's monster man-paws could wrap around her waist and pick her up like a twig. Marco was, like, all tough and quiet. He was in a gang with his older brothers and uncles. They're house had, like, three bedrooms and eight people living there. That didn't stop them from partying almost every night of the week. In the morning, their living room was covered in bodies. Imagine stumbling over that shit, trying to take a piss in the middle of the night.

Gina, on the other hand, came from the ritzy part of town. I think she dated the bad boys to tick off her dad. He was a lawyer or something, and I never saw him without a phone attached to his ear. Gina took advantage of his busyness and made up excuses to squeeze cash out of him on the fly.

Gina was always flush and paid for any of the treats we fancied. Pizza, burgers, slushies, and enough candy to make us sick was always available because of Gina's daddy wad.

Gina even paid for Marco most of the time. It wasn't her money, so she gave freely knowing she could get more any time she batted her eyes and played sweet.

Marco sold drugs to burnouts in middle school, but I don't think he made much money at it. In order to show he was one of the guys, Gina would front Marco some money to pay for our share of the party supplies.

Gina was down to do most every drug depending on her mood. She'd take pills with cough syrup and finish with a joint to keep the mix mellow.

I was too afraid of my grandma catching me glassy-eyed or smelling like a roach, so I stuck to the liquor. My favorite was this, like, candy-sweet wine. I had to be careful because the bottle had a tendency to slip down my throat way too quickly.

I would only go on benders with Gina during the weekend. Grandma's strict curfew of eight PM on weeknights prevented me from becoming a total boozer loser. But, Friday night I'd tell Grandma I was sleeping over with Gina (not a total lie), and we'd usually be found among the masses on the living room floor the next day.

I don't know what Gina told her parents to get out. Usually, they were decked out for a night on the town themselves, so I don't know how much they noticed she was gone.

Whenever Marco could get a bedroom, I was left to fend for myself among a group of much older boys. I think being between seventh and eighth grade was enough of a turnoff for most of them not to creep on me. When one of the boys would get out of pocket, somebody would straighten them out with a punch to the arm, "Dude, she's only thirteen."

I made sure to attend Mass every Sunday with Grandma to keep up appearances. And, all was well in Margaritaland.

June 11, 2010 8:20 PM

Visiting my mom in the county jail was super depressing. The first time I saw her, we had to sit on opposite sides of a thick piece of glass and talk through a metal hole and shit. It was super fucking hard to hear what she said because it was all echoey and shit. We realized that we had to sit really close and one of us had to turn our ear to the screen to hear. It made things really awkward because several times we didn't know that the other person was done talking, and we kept having these pauses, and I even forgot what the fuck we were talking about once because I got so sick of that shit.

My grandma wouldn't take me every Sunday, so the next time I got to see my ma, she'd made her way out of the cage. Evidently, if you go a month on good behavior, some of the privileges improve. We got to meet in, like, a cafeteria or something. A bunch of families were sitting around tables and talking. Some were playing cards. Some were over by the TV that was mounted to the wall and covered by a grate. I mean, if you don't get to see each other, why would they watch TV during their time together, Charlie?

I ran to my mom to give her a hug, but was immediately screamed at by an officer, "No touching!" He pounded a sign on the wall with a closed fist that said the same shit.

I guess they didn't want families passing shit back and forth. But, God damn, Charlie. They gave me the roughest fucking pat-down I've ever had. I mean this football looking bitch practically lifted me off the ground when she grabbed my legs. She made me pull my bra out and shake out my shirt. I think she even cupped my ass, Charlie. Are they allowed to do that?

Even after turning me over and shaking me around, I still can't touch my mom because I might have pulled out something from up my ass.

That's fucked up.

I kept a journal about the shit that happened to me while my mom was locked up. I'd bring in the journal to make sure to share the whole play-by-play, so she wouldn't miss a thing.

She told me she was gonna be locked up at least three or four months because she had to wait for her court date. She could've waited at home, but nobody had the cash to bond her out. My grandma could've put up her house, but something about that spooked Grandma, and when I asked, Grandma brushed me off, saying, "Maggie, now don't start talking about things you simply don't understand."

Mom looked funny while she was locked up. I mean, they didn't give her any make-up or hair products. She told me, "Who do I have to impress anyway?"

But, after a couple weeks, she started looking healthier. Her eyes seemed lighter and less puffy. Her face filled out a little bit because she'd been eating regularly. I think being on a normal schedule, instead of working nights, was doing her some good.

She said she was dying in there and hated that Uncle Larry had to cover our rent. But, she also said she'd been going back to church and even reading the Bible. She said she liked reading Job because that dude went through some fucked up shit, and it all worked out in the end because he kept believing in God the whole time. I think my mom used the time and the quiet to talk to God. I think it made her calm and gave her hope.

I'm sorry, Charlie. I just don't know. Sorry for being so emotional.

My grandpa and Christian knew God. Grandma and Mom wanted desperately to believe that some kind of goodness was out there in the world.

I just can't wrap my head around a God who loves us but then lets our uncles abuse us . . . and haunt us.

It never fucking ends, Charlie. I still have nightmares about that shit.

If we are God's children, Doc, where the fuck is He when that shit's going down.

June 15, 2010 7:30 PM

Everybody was super surprised when Justin popped up at the end of the summer. His dad was being moved overseas, and dad felt that Justin had been reformed enough to stay with his mom. Justin's dad made sure to let him know that he'd drag Justin's ass across the ocean if he ever fucked up again. And, Justin believed him.

I could tell Gina was totally uncomfortable with having both her beaus around. Even dim Marco could tell something was up and confronted Justin about it, saying, "We gonna have a problem here?"

Justin smoothed everything over by replying, "Nah, Big Homie. You can have my sloppy seconds any time."

Everyone laughed, and even Marco smirked. I think Marco's slow ass didn't know how badly Justin had just burned him. It didn't matter because all was well.

Straight out, Justin had his eyes on me. I was completely oblivious to it though.

Because he had just got back, it seemed like there was a constant line to wait in to talk to him. I didn't even bother because I never knew him from before.

I mean, don't get me wrong. Justin was hot as hell. Always wearing wife-beater tank tops, showing off those skinny ass bumps for arms and boney shoulders. I just wanted to lick from that boney collarbone, up his neck and give him another piercing in his ear with my teeth.

For some reason, his pasty white ass melted my panties. But, he was two years older than me, so I didn't I have a chance. Or, so I thought.

At first, I thought Justin was just getting the lay of the land. He had this way about him like he was running for mayor or something and wanted to shake everyone's hand and know everyone's name. I thought I was just another one of the votes for him to take over as leader of our click.

But, then Justin spent more and more time sitting next to me. I figured that it was just luck of the draw, but I later learned Justin didn't do anything by accident.

On one casual occasion, Justin slickly slipped his arm behind me, and that was it. I was all his.

Not a word was uttered. I was just whisked into the queen seat of Justin's new kingdom. He used my waste and jean loops to guide me here, there, and everywhere. And, I was just fucking enchanted, Charlie.

Now that I think about it, Justin didn't talk to me much. I was always by his side, but his head was on a swivel. He was always in, like, two or three conversations at once, keeping the party going.

I didn't have shit to say, so I'd just wrap his gangly arm around my neck and feel solid there.

June 19, 2010 6:50 PM

One drunk party night in a backyard filled with Tiki torches, things kind of hit a lull and got really quiet. I could hear some bugs and shit chirping in the dark, and a couple of bodies were littered about the backyard, settling in for the night. Gina and Marco had booked it earlier and left me to fend for myself.

Justin looked out at the tatters of a party well done and took a long draw from our bottle of candy wine. Then, he turned to me with a tipsy glint in his eye and a smirk that scrunched up the left side of his face.

"Hey."

That was all it took, Charlie. One word.

I don't know who made the first move, but the next thing I knew, we were trying to swallow each other. We moved, or fell, to the ground, and Justin straddled me on the grass, and we kissed over, and over, and over again.

I remember feeling his hard cock rubbing up against my jeans. I was terrified that he was going to undo my pants there and then and ravage me. But, as we kissed, a part me wanted him to burst through his pants and into me. I wanted him to grab my ass, my waste, my legs and to force himself deep inside me until I screamed.

I don't remember passing out. I thought the excitement would never end. But, when I woke up, the sun was out, and Justin was leaning on his elbow, just staring at me.

June 22, 2010 7:25 PM

I did it, Charlie! I can't believe I fucking did it!

Look at that . . . right there.

General . . . Education . . . Diploma.

After so many months of fucking studying. I can't believe this shit is real!

The State is Proud to Award this General Education Diploma to . . . Margarita . . . Rosa . . . GONZALEZ!!!

Aww hell. I'm so excited.

We gotta tear the roof off this mug tonight, Charlie!

Margarita's going to COLLEGE, bitches!!!

June 24, 2010 8:05 PM

The start of eighth grade was probably the most depressing school year I'd ever had.

Christian's crew moved on to high school which was good because I didn't have to be constantly reminded of the dream life I'd lost. But, that also meant my girl Gina was moving on up too. I didn't have anyone to liven the place up with pranks.

Even though bitch-boy Benny wasn't there to torcher me, I still headed to the library for lunch. The cafeteria was just too fucking noisy, and all the moving people kinda freaked me out. I didn't have anyone to see in there anyway. And, sitting alone would make me look like even more of a loser than I already did.

Ms. Swanson welcomed me back to the library with a warm smile. She never asked any questions. Just opened her doors for me to stay as long as I needed.

Justin, Gina, and Marco all went to Wabash High School. Saying they went there sounds like they were getting an education which was far from the case.

Marco really got into the drugs he and the gang were selling. He was blitzed almost every night and rarely emerged from the party palace in time to catch the bus. Most days that he went, he'd have to have somebody drop him off by third or fourth period where he'd be just in time to meet up with Gina for lunch.

Of course, he was constantly truant (probably had more detentions than he could possibly serve), but he didn't give a shit as long as he wasn't arrested for it. Marco was never gonna graduate. He only went to school to keep the heat off of his house. His time wasn't wasted though because his gang supplied the school.

Gina kept up appearances as well as she could which was quite a feat. She was with Marco as much as humanly possible but had a weeknight curfew of ten and needed to keep a "B" average to keep her parents off her case. She'd bust her ass in study hall and on the bus rides, so she'd be free to chill after school. Gina also kept her weekday partying to a minimum to make it through.

Justin was like some mad genius or something. He never carried a book and did, like, zero homework. But, he skated by with "C's" and "B's," and his mom was happy to let it slide.

Justin mainly just went to high school to gather up the burnouts and the tweakers. He'd be chummy to lure these losers into his and Marco's drug trade (Marco's crew would supply the goods, but Justin was a master salesman). I think these guys thought they were gonna party with us or something.

That was, like, Justin's ploy. But Justin would use his job at the local grocery store as cover. The dope fiends would come in, and Justin would nod them over to a corner or storeroom where they'd make the exchange.

The job kept these tweakers from getting too familiar with Justin, and it was a good cover for when Justin had to pay insurance on his car and shit. Justin was never home, so his mom didn't know how much he was working and what kind of bankroll he had. She was good with getting her money and thinking it was legit.

June 27, 2010 8:35 PM

My mom got out of jail a couple of weeks into eighth grade. The judge let her out with, like, eighteen months of house arrest. The lawyer told Grandma Rosie to bring me to the courtroom for the plea. Mom talked about wanting to be able to "raise her daughter" (me), and I think me being there in my Sunday's finest was the icing on the cake.

How was this judge gonna throw my mom back in jail right in front of me. She'd already been gone over three months.

I thought me and my main-girl Mom were gonna have some bonding time when she got released, but that never really happened, Charlie. Mom got her job back at the factory working the night shift, so our hours didn't match up well.

Jail changed my mom. Our one time that overlapped was breakfast, which would have been her dinner. After jail, she started every day by making us some sort of hot breakfast with fruit and shit. She told me having the hot breakfasts in the county really helped her think, so she figured it would help me in school.

Not much was said during these times because I was still asleep, and mom was winding down.

Now, Mom had to work on Friday nights, so that was Margarita's night to go butt-fucking wild. That's when I first started smoking weed because I didn't have to worry about anyone at home. All I had to do was be home by five AM, take a shower, and get to bed before mom rolled in.

I don't think I ever would have started smoking if not for Gina. She knew I was too goody-goody. One night she got fed up and said, "You gotta fuckin loosen up, Rita," before blowing a cloud of smoke right in my face.

A couple minutes after I got over my coughing my lungs out, this complete calm settled over me. Whenever I'd go to these parties, I was paranoid as fuck. I worried my grandma or mom would find out. I was worried the police would bust it up. I was even worried a rumor or reputation would follow me to school and my teachers would think I was a lost cause.

But, those thoughts went up in a cloud of smoke when I was around that herb, Charlie. I even slept better. A couple of blunts were enough to chase Larry away, if just for the night.

I was delirious most Saturday mornings, either drunk, high, exhausted or all of the above. Mom never seemed to notice because she got in the habit of nursing a forty before she'd pass out on the couch. I'd usually help her to bed before going back to bed myself.

Mom got right back to her old tricks, partying on the weekends with Larry. Mom was on house arrest, so to get fucked up, she'd have to have the party at our apartment. She'd pay Larry to pick up boatloads of booze and even feed Larry's coke habit. Mom felt she owed Larry for paying our rent, and she was resolved to pay him back one shot or snort at a time.

I had to go back to Grandma Rosie's for these nights. Grandma seemed to be cool with Justin, but she insisted I be back by ten. This kept the Saturday parties light and let me recover from the previous night.

I was fresh and cheery on Sunday morning to sit next to Grandma in the front row of church. And, all was well.

June 29, 2010 6:45 PM

The routine got to be pretty regular, and I started to appreciate the ins and outs of this new life. I used school to recover and rest up for our nightly mayhem. I smoked almost daily to level me out and sleep. Friday was my big bender day and Saturday was reserved for Mom to get her party on. And, Grandma Rosie still thought I was her little angel.

That is until Justin fucked it all up.

We had made out a couple of times, and once, Justin even felt me up.

I was in way over my head. I didn't know what I was doing, but it didn't seem to matter. Justin was in control and getting no complaints from me.

A couple times, I noticed my panties were wet, and I'd thought I'd pissed myself when I was drunk. But, now I know better.

Life came crashing down after Justin hit it and quit me at Renee's party.

I'd tried to call him the next day, but he never picked up. I called Gina, and she had to be the one who let me down. She said that Justin told Marco I was just too young and immature to hang with their group, and he had to let me go.

I never told Gina about him sleeping with me because Justin was her ex, and that woulda been super weird.

All at once, I was completely alone. My connection to my entire social group was through Justin. I didn't see any of them at school, and Justin was my ride to the party.

I did still hang out with Gina here and there when she needed a break from Marco. She even tried to bring me to a party once, but Justin avoided me all night, looking away from me every time I'd try to catch his eye. He ended up draping his arm around some other bitch, and I nearly lost my shit, Charlie.

I just sat in the corner, drinking alone, and decided to hoof it back home by myself around eleven.

I even tried to have a girls' night one Friday to save what was left of my pathetic social life. I told Gina to invite some of her friends and bring weed. I'd supply the booze from Mom's enormous stash. She wasn't gonna notice.

It was just Gina and two other bitches. The other two were just there to pre-party before going to Marco's, and they left before nine.

Gina and I shared a roach, and I blurted out all the depressed shit I was going through. I think Gina felt for me, but we'd been drifting apart since the summer ended. There wasn't anything Gina could do for me. She had her own tornado to deal with trying to balance slummin it with Marco and the richy-rich house she lived in.

Gina left around eleven. That was pretty much it for us.

I was all alone.

July 2, 2010 6:35 PM

I didn't mind being alone, Charlie. I really didn't. I had nothing better to do, so my grades really improved for a while there.

But, without any other distractions, my mind fucked me over.

Getting to sleep was impossible. Every time I'd nod off, Larry would run up on me immediately. I tried watching TV and reading books to distract my mind. But, as soon as my eyes got heavy, Larry'd be right there.

I got so worked up and paranoid that I even latched the chain on our apartment door one night. It must have worked to help me sleep because I woke up to my mom pounding and hissing through the cracked door because she couldn't get in in the morning.

"What the fuck's wrong with you, Rita?" Mom wasn't happy, and I lied that I kept hearing footsteps in the hall.

At that moment, I think my mom realized what a little girl I was. Her face dropped, and she might have been crying. She told me to get ready for school and made my favorite breakfast, waffles with strawberries. Mom even let me put whip cream on it, which she never did.

She stopped me before I left to hug me and give me a kiss on the head, saying, "You know how proud I am of you, don't you?"

July 5, 2010 7:10 PM

The only place I could get consistent shuteye was on the bus or at school because Larry had never been there. I took as much advantage of the bus rides and free periods as I could. The bell was usually a good alarm, but the bus driver regularly had to wake me up because none of the other assholes passing my seat bothered.

The driver was some sort of snitch because he got the school to call my mom a couple of times. I wasn't in trouble or anything, but the school and my mom were worried. I told Mom I was fine, and she told the school I must be going through a growth spurt or something.

I don't know how everyone else stayed awake in our puffy winter coats and the blasts of warm air on the bus. Even if I was sleeping at night, I'd still probably nod off here and there.

I looked like shit the second half of eighth grade. I had to apply a boatload of concealer to hide the dark circles around my eyes. I knew I couldn't keep going this way.

I contacted Gina to get her to bring me some weed. She wasn't a regular dealer. I think that was where she drew the line. Her parents could forgive a lot of sins, but if she got caught, being labeled a drug dealer would push it too far.

Marco gave her what she needed, and she'd give it to me for the regular price. She never asked Marco or me for a cut. She must have seen how I was wasting away.

I could barely keep my already baggy clothes from falling off. Even my tighter clothes billowed out. My cheeks were sucked in and even my boobs and ass shrunk.

I was just never hungry, Charlie. If I ever got a second to myself, I'd fall asleep. Eating was a hazard because I'd face plant or choke.

Things got a little better with the weed. I'd started by smoking in my room and blowing out the window. But, I froze my ass off, and the cold wind blew most of the smoke back into my room. I'd had to use, like, half a bottle of air freshener to get the smell out. I could still smell it every once in a while for a couple of weeks.

Since it was dark and cold, I'd take a walk down our back ally just after mom left for work. My puffs of smoke looked like steam, and I could tuck the joint into my coat sleeve. I just had to be careful not to burn my coat. I ended up getting a couple of marks on both sleeves, but you couldn't see them from the outside, so we were all good.

Mom appreciated me taking care of the laundry because I'd have to wash my coat and clothes every night when I got back. I even threw in my mom's clothes every once in a while. She called me "responsible" for taking on some chores.

It broke my heart to see the pride in her eyes, knowing I wasn't being good. I was just a hype.

The only catch was remembering to put the clothes in the dryer. After getting high was the only time I was hungry. I'd eat 'til I was about to bust and slept great.

I only forgot to switch the clothes once, leaving me with no coat to go to school. Despite having my hoody pulled down tight, I shivered for, like, a full hour when I got to school.

July 9, 2010 8:35 PM

I think at one point I became a dope fiend, Charlie.

My weeks were going great because I'd smoke, eat, and then sleep like a baby. My face, booty, and boobs thickened out, and I even became more hopeful. I heard some, like, really educated potheads talking about how much marijuana heals and shit, and brother, I'm a believer.

The only times I couldn't smoke were on the weekends. I was at Grandma's on Saturday, and Mom was around on Sunday.

On the Sundays, if Mom wasn't too hurtin from a hangover, she'd take me to see a late afternoon movie. It was a way to bond that didn't require much effort, and she could pass out if the mood struck her, which it frequently did.

Either way, I couldn't go around reeking of weed with those two around.

When I got into a good groove, I really found myself missing the bud when I couldn't have it. Sleeping at

Grandma's was literally a nightmare because that room was where Larry had gotten after me.

I tried sneaking some of my Mom's booze over to Grandma's in water bottles. When Grandma turned in for the night, I turned to the vodka or rum. I hated the way it burned my throat and my belly, but I was too scared to go downstairs and get some juice to mix it with.

I'd usually give up drinking too soon, and Larry would chase me through the night. I was drunk enough to sleep but not, like, blackout drunk where I wouldn't have to dream

I talked to Gina about it when she came with my weekly delivery. I told her I needed something to get through the boring time at my grandma's (only a partial lie). She suggested a couple anxiety pills, and she pulled a bag of four out of her pocket. She said she'd pop one or two when she needed to escape from wherever she was but couldn't risk smoking up.

The pills worked great! I took one after Grandma nodded off, and it only took like thirty minutes until I was feeling no pain. I slept like a baby and didn't wake up until like 9:30 the next day. Grandma took me to the last church service at eleven because I'd slept so late, and she was worried I was sick.

151

July 12, 2010 7:05 PM

We had a good thing going there for a while, Charlie. I'd smoke, eat, sleep during the week, and pop a pill on the weekends. I found the pills made the movies with Mom so much more enjoyable. That is, unless I passed out right next to Mom. Mom mentioned something about not paying so much for us to take nap, but I told her it was a onetime thing, so we'd go back the next weekend. I saved my snoozy pill for later at night, and we were all good.

I didn't want to oversleep church and raise suspicions, so I got good at popping a pill when I'd brush my teeth and change for bed. I timed it out right to be getting loopy at just about the same time Grandma Rosie was nodding off. One of us would nudge the other, and we'd trudge to bed together.

One night, I fell sound asleep on the couch. Like, full sawing a log style, Charlie. Grandma had to shake me a few times to bring me back, and I was so confused that I didn't know where I was and what time it was and even what day it was.

I think I stumbled my way up to bed, but I don't remember that journey.

I don't know if Larry had been trying to get back after me for a while or what, but he took advantage of that perfect opportunity.

I heard him in my dreams which hadn't happened in a while.

"Riiita . . . Oh, Riiiiiitaaa . . . Wakey, wakey. Rise and shine."

I came to with Larry leaning with one hand against the wall to steady himself right next to my bed. His pants were already at his knees and his curved dick was staring me in the face. I jumped back, thinking it was gonna shoot all over me.

Larry had a nasty grin from ear to ear. "You thought you were so smart, Little Margarita, blocking the door all those nights. But, I knew. I knew you'd make a mistake at some point. And, here I am," Larry brought his beer to his smiling, pursed lips.

"See the problem is I've been jonesing for your little, Latina ass for way too long, Honey. If you'd just given me a nibble here or there, we wouldn't have this throbbing, hard problem. But, every time I tried to sneak in your room and the door would catch, my poor ole balls just got bluer and bluer.

"Just looking at you there with your little headlights rubbing against that t-shirt has me fit to burst. The problem is Ole Larry is probably too drunk to jerk off.

I'm gonna need you to help your Uncle Larry out a little bit."

Charlie, I was paralyzed. I think, at first, I thought it was another nightmare. But, I couldn't wake up.

Larry grabbed my leg and pulled to the edge of the bed. "Now, don't be shy. Just give my friend here a little tug, will ya?"

I'd never touched a penis before, Charlie, outside of maybe Justin grinding on me during a make out session. I had no fucking clue what to do with what was staring me in the eye.

I don't know if I was still stoned or thought I was dreaming, but when Larry grabbed my hand and started guiding it along his cock, I just kept going with his rhythm. He'd wrapped my hand around it just the way he liked it and got the motion going. I think I figured if I kept going, he'd just finish and leave, but that shit felt like it lasted forever.

Evidently, I give a pretty good hand job because Larry was moaning and convulsing and shit. I had to stand up off the bed to get the right angle to tug the way Larry wanted me to, and Larry took this as an invitation to lean on me with one hand to steady himself.

As things were close to wrapping up, Larry leaned in to rest his chin on my shoulder and stare down my back. He put his beer on the nightstand to use his free hands to pull down the back of my pants. I wouldn't let go of his cock for fear he'd try to plunge into me. But, Pervy Larry just wanted a peek at that ass he'd been missing so much.

Without warning, Larry unloaded on my hip and thigh. He kinda quivered and backed away. I wasn't sure when to let go, and my hand was drenched in that sticky goo. He pulled up his pants and buttoned them, not bothering to zip his fly or do his belt. He grabbed his beer and reached in his pocket. He pulled out a wadded up ten dollar bill and two singles. He said, "Don't say I never gave you nothin," and threw the crumpled up bills off my shoulder and walked out.

July 20, 2010 8:45 PM

Sorry that I haven't wanted to talk, Charlie. You've really helped me out, but I think I let my guard down a little too far last time. I've never told anybody about the time Larry made me jerk him off.

I think I was too ashamed.

I still think it was my fault. If I wasn't so stoned and groggy, I'd have blocked the door like I usually did. But, stupid me passed out and left the door unguarded.

I wanted to kill myself that night, Charlie. I took the only two pills I had left from Gina. I don't know how I thought they'd help me, but I just couldn't stop shaking.

The door was still open. I was frozen on my bed in the corner staring at it. I could feel Larry's jiz spreading down my hip to make a puddle under my ass.

The drugs wanted to bring me down and drown it out, but every time my eyes got heavy and my head would bob, I'd jolt back awake in terror.

I started sobbing and shaking, but I didn't want to be too loud because Larry or Grandma might hear.

I couldn't escape this nightmare.

After I don't know how long, I gathered myself enough to grab my stash of weed and head out the door. I never left my shit at home because I didn't know what somebody might find during my Mom's epic drunk fests.

I lit a joint and nearly inhaled the whole fucking thing in one go. After a coughing fit, I finished it and threw the roach away.

I didn't know what to do or where to go. The thought of going back to Grandma's made me want to throw up. I didn't know what time it was and wasn't sure if Mom would still be in the middle of her bender. I didn't know how she'd react, and I definitely didn't want her asking questions.

I pulled my hood over my head and did a lap of Grandma's block, making sure to pass by her house on the other side of the street when I came back around. As my thinking cleared a little, I figured I'd swing by the apartment to see if the party had died down. If the coast was clear, I'd sneak into bed.

I don't know how far I got before the mix of weed and pills hit me, but all at once, I became, like, super numb. I don't remember if I was still walking toward my apartment or what the fuck was going on, but at some point a car pulled up to the curb next to where I was walking.

"Can I give you a lift home?" this chiseled guy with a killer smile asked me from his rolled down window. He had a leather jacket, a button up shirt that opened at the top, and some jeans that hugged his tight ass just right.

I don't know what I was thinking, but I was definitely feeling no pain. I tried to turn on the charm and asked him, "You lookin for a good time, Big Boy? I'll relieve some of the tension in those tight pants for twenty bucks."

The sweetness drained from his face as he dropped his head toward the steering wheel. "I wish you wouldn't have said that." He flicked a button and bright lights started flashing. "Put your hands on the car," he directed me without ever looking my way.

I don't know if I tried to turn and run or was just startled by the siren, but I face-planted in the grass next to the car. I didn't want to get shot, so I just lay there, face down, with my hands on my head. The police officer put handcuffs on me, lifted me up, and put me in the back of his car.

I fucking passed out on the way to the police station, Charlie.

July 22, 2010 6:45 PM

When I finally emerged from my haze, Officer Friendly was shaking me, and some medic with rubber gloves was flashing a light in my face. The medic and Friendly kept asking, "What did you take? Hey, what are you on?"

"Some pills," I told them.

"Some pills?" They repeated. I don't think my speech was all that clear. My tongue felt like it had swelled up and was getting in the way of my words. "What kind of pills?"

"Anxiety."

"Anxiety? What kind? . . ." the medic listed a whole bunch of names I had never heard of. As I was trying to think, I wasn't ever sure if Gina told me what they were.

"Are you on anything else?" the medic asked.

"I found these joints on you," Officer Friendly helpfully tried to jog my memory.

"I had one joint."

"One joint?" The medic mirrored my answers. "Some anxiety pills and one joint? Anything else?"

I shook my head. Yes or no questions were much preferred in my state.

"We're gonna have to draw some blood to make sure you're not in danger of overdosing. Most likely you partied a little too hard this evening. We'll get you some fluids and you'll have to sleep it off." Sleep sounded fantastic, and before I knew it, I'd taken his advice and drifted away.

I felt the pinch when they inserted the needle, but I didn't even bother to look down.

July 24, 2010 7:10 PM

I wouldn't say I woke up so much as I emerged. It felt like my soul had to come up into my body, and as my eyes opened and I lifted my head, it felt like my body and soul weren't fully connected yet.

"Good morning, Sleeping Beauty. Or, should I say good afternoon? It's almost five o'clock."

I stared toward the grey blob that was talking to me, and slowly, a uniformed guard came into view. I put my hand on my head to steady myself and jog my memories, "Where am I?"

The guard connected the dots. "You, my dear, are in our fine lock up. Don't move too quickly because they still have got that needle in your arm. Just sit tight, and I'll call the nurse."

I slowly realized there were bars between me and my helpful new friend. I was laying on a cot and a needle connected from my arm to a half-full bag of something next to the bed. Whatever it was, I was grateful that I didn't have a pounding hangover.

Under the bag was a box that had a couple of green numbers that changed every couple of seconds. I was startled into being fully awake when some band on my arm tightened. It released, letting air out, and a beep caused a bunch of the numbers to change.

"Well hello there," a sweet, plump, middle aged women in green scrubs greeted me. "I'm Nurse Williams. I work here at the precinct. You gave us a little scare last night. How are you feeling now?" She smiled and looked deep into my eyes as if she wanted nothing more than to hear what I had to say.

That look made me think she'd have waited as long as I needed to get a response together, and it threw me off a little. I forgot I was supposed to say something until the guard in grey started shifting a little. "Oh, I'm fine.

Things are a little foggy. I don't quite remember how I got here. You didn't call my mom did you?"

"Not yet, Dear." I nearly overdosed and got arrested, but this nurse was an angel to me. I still don't get why she was so sweet, Charlie. "We need some of your details to contact somebody for you." She asked me my name, age, phone number, address, Mom's name and some other shit before saying, "You just sit tight, and we'll get your mom for you."

I don't know what kind of state I was in, Charlie, but that sing-songy nurse had me thinking everything was going to be just fine.

July 28, 2010 6:50 PM

Everything was not alright, Charlie.

They couldn't find my mom. They tried calling her over and over. After a couple of hours, they asked me if there was someone else they could call, but I wasn't about to get Grandma Rosie involved. It would have broken her heart. Plus, Larry might have driven her over, and that would've just topped the shit sandwich I was already in.

Some lawyer came to talk to me, and the guard asked me to turn around and stick my hands out of the cell. It wasn't until the cuffs were clicked in place that I realized how deep of shit I was in.

The guard kept a hand wrapped around my upper arm as he led me to a small room with a small table, one chair, and a bench along the wall with a bar above it. The guard told me to sit on the bench and uncuffed one wrist to attach that cuff to the metal bar. Then the guard left.

"Hello, Margarita. I'm Mr. Spencer, your lawyer." This pudgy, sweaty, balding, white dude extended a hand to me. I tried to shake it out of reflex, but my right hand jerked back to the metal poll I was connected to. I gave Mr. Spencer my left hand, and we got off to an awkward start.

I tried to listen to what he had to say, but I kept getting distracted by the mirror behind him. I interrupted, "is somebody watching us?"

"No, no, no Ms. Gonzalez, police can't observe an attorney, client conversation. Everything we say here is protected." He mustered an awkward smile. "Now, I need you to listen because you're in a bit of trouble. You solicited a police officer, had multiple illicit drugs in your system, and they found three marijuana joints on your person. You're facing some serious charges."

This guy was talking way too fast for me. "Wait, wait, I did what to a police officer?"

"Solicitation, Ms. Gonzalez." Mr. Spencer could tell I wasn't picking this up. "You offered him sex for money."

"Whoa, whoa, wait a minute. I never offered to have sex with the police officer." I tried to defend myself.

"So, you're saying," Mr. Spencer flipped through a note pad, "you did not tell Officer McNamara you'd 'relieve some tension in his pants for twenty dollars.'"

My face turned beat red, and I could feel some throbbing in my temples. I didn't know whether to be terrified by the charges or horribly embarrassed that I'd offered to jack off a cop. I was both.

"Well, Ms. Gonzalez, I'll see if we can get the blood test dropped because you didn't give written consent. But, you did have three joints on your person, were visibly intoxicated, admitted to taking illicit drugs, and you're not disputing that you solicited Officer McNamara." Mr. Spencer pulled out a handkerchief to wipe the sweat from his forehead. I think he was hot because his suit was definitely too small, and I could tell he couldn't get comfortable.

"This is serious, and no matter what I do, it looks like you'll be going to jail. I'll do my best to see if I can get you a plea bargain because this is your first time, but having drugs on you almost always leads to jail time." Mr. Spencer stood and extended a hand for us to awkwardly shake again. "We'll try to find your mom, but I'd prepare yourself for spending some time behind bars. Good luck, Ms. Gonzalez."

August 2, 2010 8:35 PM

Charlie, I had to fucking strip butt-ass naked in front of some big ole, black bitch. This police officer had blue rubber gloves on and watched me strip before giving me this flimsy, papery plastic covering. I thought I was gonna rip it in half when I pulled it over my head.

Then came the fun. This bitch told me to bend forward, spread my butt cheeks, and cough several times. I had to lift the paper dress, so she could get a good look up my ass.

I started crying when she came around in front of me and went down on one knee to tell me to thrust forward, spread my cooch open, and cough again. She had a fucking flashlight, Charlie. She was fucking exploring my holes, searching for gold with a fucking flashlight. When I thrust to give her a good peak, the dried Larry jiz that was still on my right ass cheek pulled at my skin.

That had to be the lowest point of my life, Charlie. Violated, arrested, and violated again.

I got to take a shower after we were done. I thought being clean and trying to start fresh was going to pick me up. And, it did for a little while. But, I found out later that any hope I'd had of making Larry pay for what he'd done was washed right down the drain.

August 5, 2010 7:25 PM

All new youth inmates are given a blue jumpsuit. It's all one-piece with long pants and long sleeves and a zipper down to the belly button. I was given a t-shirt, sports bra, and panties to go under the jump suit.

They put a chain around my waste that had handcuffs attached, so my hands were never more than six inches away from my body. The leg chains were set farther apart, so I could walk. And for some reason, there was a chain connecting the leg irons up to my waistband by my bellybutton. For the life of me, I can't figure out why you needed that extra chain. Even a magician couldn't wiggle out of that shit.

I boarded a van that had steel grates to protect the two guards sitting up front from little old me, and we headed to the Juvenile Detention Center or JDC as we like to call it.

I couldn't stay in the city lockup any longer. They told me it had already been thirty-six hours, and my mom still wasn't answering any of the numbers I gave them. If she called back they would tell her who to call at the JDC.

Since I was just a little girl, I couldn't be in a city cell with anyone else, so the other cells got a little cramped during my stay. I found out that if any of the men, who regularly cat-called at me, would've gotten in a fight in their cell, there wouldn't have been another place to put them. And, that made our jailers a little edgy.

At the JDC, I was briefed by my intake counselor that I'd have to go through a number of tests and screenings before I could be assigned a living unit. She said the process would take about a week, and I'd have to live in an intake area and wouldn't be able to go to school or anything until they "classified" me.

Though I was separated from the rest of the girls, I could see some of them through different windows as I walked the halls. When I'd pass by, a couple would run up to get a better look at me. A few howled and yelled some perverted shit at me, "Mmmmm, back that thang up, bitch!" One or two stared me down and made threats like, "Fresh meat! I'm gonna beat yo bitch ass!"

I didn't know why somebody would want to fight just by looking at someone else, but I was terrified to leave the safety of the intake dorm.

My little dorm was a perfect home for a week. I had one neighbor for a little over a day, but she was pushed into the general population. As for me, I had the six rooms surrounding a small room that had a circular table with four chairs branching from a center pole all to myself.

There was an old, clunky TV mounted up in one corner, but we did have cable, Charlie. The officers assigned to me would usually let me pick the station. Sometimes, negotiating was involved. But, for the most part, all the officers were very nice to me.

Since there was no one else around, the officers would talk to me. I got to tell a couple different versions of my background to different people. I liked Officer Kelly the most. I don't know if that was her first name or last name, but she was young and pretty and sweet, and she asked me deep questions and really, like, listened and offered me advice. I think she was the best part of those five lonely days.

For most of the time, we'd play card games or checkers or chess to pass the time. Every once in a while the guards would have to do some paperwork or make phone calls, and I'd retreat to my bed to read a book or take a nap.

I really appreciated the time I had to myself to clear my head and rest. I didn't realize how hectic my life had gotten until I couldn't go anywhere or do anything and had to sit there with my thoughts. I figured I was safe from Larry for the time being, so I just slept a lot to make up for lost time.

August 8, 2010 7:05 PM

During the days, I didn't get much time to lounge. Once in the morning and once after lunch, somebody would grab me and give me a tour or a test.

I had to take a drug assessment because I came in high, and they found my stash. The drug counselor determined I had a problem even though I told them I just used in order to sleep. I didn't tell them why I couldn't sleep. I didn't tell anybody about Larry.

I took academic tests, and the person testing me said I did pretty well, and they'd put me in the high group at school. Whatever that meant.

There was one counselor lady who asked me a shit-ton of sex questions. Had I given oral sex; had I received oral sex; had I had anal sex; had I put anything up my ass? I was horribly embarrassed by the questions, Charlie. Did this bitch think I was a sex fiend? I guess, based on the charges, she probably thought I was a prostitute or something.

I told her I'd only had sex one time, and I didn't know if he wore a condom which was the truth. I don't think that response would have helped my drug test because I was passed out for the sex. I don't think this lady believed me because I got picked up for soliciting a cop.

I mean, would you have believed me, Doc? The story I was selling is that the first time I offered someone sex for money, I just happened to be bombed out of my mind, and that person happened to be a cop.

I know why that bitch didn't trust me. I don't blame her.

For my second to last day of intake, I got to get all shackled up to get in a van that drove me to the other fucking side of the parking lot, so I could go before the judge.

The dude in the robe read me all the charges they trumped up on me. My lawyer said not to worry because some would be thrown out or combined. Each joint had its own charge, Charlie. So, I had like 3 counts of possession. I also got charged with public intoxication and attempted suicide.

Number one, I don't think I was really trying to kill myself. And, number two, I didn't know failed suicide was a fucking crime. That's like literally insult on top of fucking injury.

The judge said I'd have to post a 50,000 dollar bail to get out of jail before the trial. My judge explained I'd have to put up 5,000 in cash and use some sort of property to cover the rest. That way, if I didn't show to court, they could take Grandma Rosie's house.

At this point, they still hadn't reached my mom, and it had been a week. Evidently, Grandma Rosie had called the police station just after I left, but they didn't tell her anything because they couldn't verify that she was a guardian or something.

Grandma Rosie did tell them that my mom was in jail as well. Get this, Charlie. Mom was in the same fucking jail as me, and nobody fucking knew it.

Well, the local police station fucking fumbled the message or something because it took another couple of days for word to get to my counselor and for her to get me a phone call with Mom.

I asked Mom what fucking happened. She said that some neighbor complained about the noise from the party. Since Mom's name was on the lease, when the police looked things up, it showed Mom was on parole for assaulting a cop.

Shit hit the fan after that. Two squads rolled up, and four officers came barging through the door. Everybody was arrested and searched, and needless to say there were plenty of party drugs on the people or in the apartment.

My mom got charged with all that shit.

Evidently, when Larry heard "Police!" he fucking jumped out my window, busting through my screen in the process. He must not have been too worried about

Mom because he had plenty of energy to get it up for me.

Mom said she was in deep shit and couldn't help me from there. Even though we were in the same fucking building, Charlie, rules said we couldn't see each other. Mom said she'd talk to her lawyer about giving Grandma Rosie temporary guardian status, so she could come to court with me.

Before we hung up, I made my counselor promise I'd get to talk to Mom again, and the counselor said we could talk once a week, but it would have to be on speaker, so she could listen in.

I got a little choked up saying goodbye. In that moment, I honestly didn't know if I'd ever see her again. We were both in some deep shit, Charlie.

I told her I loved her then got a little embarrassed because I couldn't remember the last time I said, "I love you," to my mom. I don't regret it though. It was the right thing to say.

She sniffled and said, "I love you too, Sweety." And, we heard a click.

August 12, 2010 8:20 PM

I got to greet the next, new intake girl and give her a rundown of what I knew of the system while I was packing what little shit I had to move to general pop. Her name was Jisela, and I hope I never looked as scared as she did, Charlie.

I don't think she heard a fucking word I said because she kept rubbing her hands together, and she had this far off look like she never even saw me.

I got stopped in the middle of my ten minute packing process, and Jisela was told that she had to return to her cell for a lockdown. Later, the guard told me that the men of 3A got into a huge fight in their cafeteria. We had to stay in our rooms because all available guards had to report to the third floor to get things in order.

It took a couple hours to come off lockdown status because they needed to conduct interviews and an investigation to find out who jumped who and why. Then, extra guards were needed to move this inmate here and that inmate there and process all the paperwork.

By the time the whole thing was cleared, it was past dinner time, and they decided to keep me on intake for one more night.

Even though they popped our doors to give us an hour to rec, stretch, and watch TV, Jisela never got off her bed. She kept her back to me and didn't respond to either me or Ms. Kelly when we asked her if she wanted to play cards.

Shortly after lights out was called, I heard banging coming from Jisela's room. Ms. Kelly tried to talk to her through the crack in the door, but I could tell Jisela wasn't hearing it. Ms. Kelly told me that Jisela was standing with her back against the door just kicking it over and over. Jisela didn't respond to any of the attempts Ms. Kelly made to get her to stop. Ms. Kelly called the control room for help, but they said they were still short from the fight, so if the girl wasn't hurting herself, Ms. Kelly was supposed to let it fly.

I tried holding my pillow around my ears, but the pounding was too loud to block out. After almost an hour, the pounding changed. It was more of a thud now. When Ms. Kelly checked on Jisela, she found that Jisela was sitting on the floor and banging her head backwards into the door.

Again, Ms. Kelly called control, and they had to wake up the warden and the head of the clinic to see what to do with Jisela. The clinic director called Ms. Kelly back and asked a whole bunch of questions about how hard Jisela was banging her head into the door. Did Ms. Kelly think she was in danger of a concussion or brain injury? The thuds weren't that loud, and they started to get further and further apart after a while.

Ms. Kelly ended up sitting on the ground with her face smooshed against the wall to watch Jisela bang the door over and over. Eventually, it got old, and Jisela kind of slumped to the ground and fell asleep.

I couldn't fucking sleep a wink, Charlie. That bitch was all kinds of crazy and having to watch Ms. Kelly do nothing while this girl cracked her head against the door really fucking freaked me out. I didn't think I slept at all that night, but then the door popped, and it was time for breakfast.

Jisela stood up off the floor and walked straight over to the window to the outside. She stayed there kinda resting her head against two bars that prevented our escape and stared out.

I ate my breakfast, packed my shit, and left to join the general population without saying another word to her.

Jisela didn't come to general pop. Somebody said they transferred her to a different facility, but I think that loony toon was sent straight to the nut house.

August 16, 2010 6:35 PM

Moving from intake to general pop, I had to throw what little I had into my sheet and wrap it up like a sack and carry it through several sets of clunky doors to my new dorm. See, there were doors like every ten feet to keep everyone apart. Somebody told me in that big, brick building were housed several hundred men, about a hundred women, like, seventy boys and twenty to thirty girls. So, every time we'd come to a door, the guard would call a control center on the floor we were on to ask them to pop the number that was painted on that door.

Some doors had "a" or "b" on them which meant that there could be people milling about on the other side. We'd have to go in the first door, wait in a small hall for it to close, then the second door would open. One guard told me that both these doors couldn't be opened at once to keep people from escaping.

I was assigned to Block 1A. The guard who dropped me off said the building was 5 stories tall and each story had four blocks with twenty-four rooms to a block.

The girls were spoiled because Block 1A and Block 1B were connected, so we got 48 rooms all to ourselves. No one had to pair up. 1A, where I stayed, were the younger, smaller girls, and 1B were the older, bigger, meaner looking girls. Some as old as nineteen, Charlie.

For the most part, we were kept apart from 1B. We went to lunch, had therapy groups, and rec'd by ourselves. The only time the Blocks got combined was for school.

August 20, 2010 8:05 PM

The school was the central hub for block 1A and 1B. In the middle, was a raised, box room that went half-way to the ceiling with brick and the rest was some thick ass glass. This was our control room.

Surrounding Control were four classrooms in the corners. Between the classrooms were hallways. One hall led to 1A, one led to 1B, one led to the cafeteria, and one led to our rinky-dink gym. Everyone entered and exited our section of the prison through a set of doors in the back of the gym.

Control was in the perfect place to see everything that was going on in the classrooms. They could also see down each hallway and monitor movement. A guard told me that nobody except the wardens had keys to get in the control room. The only way to get in was to be let in from the inside. Since it was supposed to be manned twenty-four-seven, not having keys made it so nobody could leave until somebody came to sub them out.

I think the guards quickly shared this info in case one of us was thinking about escaping. The guards let us know that their keys couldn't get us into control, and they couldn't get us out the last door to freedom. Both of those had to be buzzed from inside control. I thought this was a clever move because then nobody would get any ideas about jumping the guards. Most of us girls probably didn't have the guts, but I'm sure some of the men on the upper levels who were facing some serious time probably gave that a thought or two.

August 23, 2010 7:40 PM

School was six hours a day in ninety minute chunks. We'd leave 1A and circle around the control booth in one direction until we came to our class. Our guards knew if we made it back around to where we came from, they'd take our behavior points for fucking around. 1B would come in right after us and class would start. When class was done, each class would move over to the next classroom in line until we had gone to all four.

Nobody would ever officially admit that there were two high groups and two low groups for school, but that's how things ran. The groups were divided up by who was least likely to fight in class.

When I first got into class, Ms. Stewart, the language arts teacher, asked me if I'd graduated eighth grade. I told her I was going to in like a month. Ms. Stewart told me that I'd likely still be locked up until then, and that based on my test scores, I could just take the Constitution Test and start earning high school credit while I was with them.

This was a fucking bummer, Charlie. Even though my time at Mason was far from perfect, I'd worked hard enough to pass. I should've been able to get my diploma like everybody else.

I took a day to think about it, but I figured I'd better make the best of it and could get a head start on high school and maybe graduate early. So, I passed Ms. Stewart's constitution test and got a black and white certificate for that and another piece of paper that was supposed to be my eighth grade diploma.

Everybody got some version of social studies, language arts, science, and math. The school figured that each kid needed all these credits to graduate, and most of us wouldn't be here long enough to figure out what other credits we needed or to get many credits anyways. Ms. Sterwart told me that they'd give us a grade and tell our next school how much time we were in class, and our next school would give us some credits.

The teachers taught the whole class together except for math. During math, each person went at their own pace based on a pre-test the teacher, Mr. Kurface, gave us.

It was confusing as hell to start my classes because each class was, like, in the middle of a chapter. But, most of the chapters didn't last more than a couple days, and my teachers told me to just do what I could, and I'd get credit. So, I kinda got to ease my way into high school that way.

One of the other girls on 1A told me I had to "buddy up" with one of the older girls to stay out of trouble. Kina said that we'd essentially be girlfriend, girlfriend and write notes back and forth. Kina told me not to worry about having sex or making out or anything because the furthest any of the girls got was a quick brush of the arm. If anything more than that happened, we could be held back from school for up to five days, and nobody wanted to be stuck on the block that long.

I asked Kina why I needed to bother with a "girlfriend" and told her I wasn't gay. Kina said, "We're all gay for the stay," and told me the older girls just liked thinking they had a little bitch. If I had a girlfriend that meant none of the other girls would beat my ass or mess with me because I'd have an older protector and shit.

Kina gave me the low-down on which girls had been checking me out, and I decided to start writing the biggest, baddest, ugliest looking bitch because I didn't want anyone to fuck with me, and I figured if she was butt, ass ugly, then I wouldn't get confused and actually start to be gay or something.

Our fling didn't last long because that bitch was cut loose like three days later. I didn't bother pairing up with another girl because every day or so one or two people would end up leaving. I found out that most girls didn't stay more than a couple of weeks, and before long, I was one of the ones who had been there the longest which gave me some street cred with the newer bitches.

August 27, 2010 7:15 PM

I only got to spend about four weeks in the JDC because my lawyer pled me out. It took most of that time for Grandma Rosie to get the custody papers signed anyway. The agreement was that Grandma would be in charge of me until my mom was released. Then, I'd get to go live back with Mom as long as I wasn't on parole or probation.

I had to go to the courthouse again and sit in a side room with my lawyer, my grandma, the prosecutor, and a judge to sign off on my sentencing.

My lawyer got me six months because he argued I might have been kidding with the cop about giving him a handjob. In any case, no money was exchanged and the service to be performed wasn't detailed, so the prostitution charge got dropped.

Each joint of marijuana carried a six month mandatory sentence with it, but my lawyer got them to go easy and have me do all of the sentences at the same time if I admitted to being wasted when I was arrested.

My lawyer patted himself on the back and warned me that if everything would have been charged together, I could have faced five years. So, I guess I dodged a bullet there.

The judge let me know I'd have to transfer to Janesville Juvenile State Prison. The month I'd already served would be counted towards my six, so I'd only have five months left. But, when I got out, I'd be on probation until the full eighteen months of my drug sentence was over.

I didn't really know how lucky I should feel about all this, Charlie. There was nothing to go back to on the outside. I had no friends. Larry was constantly chasing after me. I was a dope fiend. And, my mom was gonna be locked up for a bit too.

I think at that point, going to prison was the best thing for me.

Janesville had the same fucking intake process that the JDC had. I had to strip again, and the county officer collected my jumpsuit and underwear in a bag before I was given the same fucking looking shit from a Janesville guard.

Evidently, because different taxes pay for the different prisons, these assholes have to protect their shitty property. The Janesville guard did get a good look up my asshole and twat during the exchange. She couldn't just take the other bitch's word that I hadn't shoved anything up there? Had to get a looksee herself.

I had to go through another intake and another bunch of tests that were almost the same as the JDC. On day two, when I pushed back, Mr. Peters, my counselor, told me it takes forever to get the files transferred over, and it's just faster for them to give us their own tests.

Bullshit.

This intake dorm at least had two other girls to spend some time with. Regina and Faith had come from a different JDC and arrived two days before me. So, we'd be spending some time together.

Regina was the lookout for her boyfriend's gang when they were robbing a convenience store. Evidently, hanging around out front, Regina was looking around too much and looked right into the security camera.

The cops easily identified her because her picture was in the system from a previous arrest for selling drugs at school. Regina refused to give up the rest of the gang, so she was sentenced for the whole thing and could be at Janesville for up to five years.

Faith was a meth head. By the time she came to Janesville, she'd already sobered up, but she said the trip down in the JDC was a fucking nightmare. She said she couldn't sleep, saw bugs crawling on her, felt like she was getting stabbed and the knife was being twisted in her stomach and chest, was always sweating or freezing, puked up anything she ate or drank and even shit the bed once.

Faith's family made meth in their garage and sold it. Her parents and older brother warned her not to try any of that shit, but curiosity got the better of her one day. Even though she'd only tried it once, the high was so powerful she couldn't stop. She kept sneaking bits away from the family stash and got caught because she was wandering down the middle of the street at midnight fucked up out of her mind.

When the cops came to check out her house, her dad tried to burn down the garage, thinking that would cover their tracks. The fire department put it out, and they

183

recovered enough evidence to put her mom and dad in jail for a long time. Her dad would have to stay longer because he had an arson charge as well.

Her brother was arrested too, but the family knew this might happen one day and told him to deny all knowledge. Mom and Dad took the rap, and sonny boy got to go free.

Even though Faith only had six months for possession, she was in no hurry to leave because she had nothing to go back to.

September 3, 2010 6:50 PM

Janesville was out in the middle of Podunk nowhere, Charlie. We had a big area that was fenced in with, like, eight foot fences and barbed wire. I don't know why anyone would try to escape anyways. You couldn't see another house in any direction you looked.

It was fun to watch the fence as night fell because the animals would come out. We'd see deer and foxes, and on one perfect night, I got to see a coyote howl at the moon.

Even though we had all this space, most of it wasn't used. Janesville let a good portion of it just become, like, a swamp and shit. They said it used to be farmland where they'd grow vegetables and corn, but the girls stopped planting and harvesting, and it became overgrown with grass and weeds.

I asked if we could get the farm back going again. I mean we had most of the summer left. The guard laughed and told me every couple of years some kid like me would want to get it started. A group of us would go out there and start weeding, but about half-way through the first day, the kids would say, "fuck it," and the farm would go another year unplanted.

Janesville had a short, blacktop basketball court with two hoops with no nets and faded paint for the out of bounds lines. The softball field looked a lot like the farm. It had a backstop and bleachers and shit, but where the dirt was supposed to be, there were more weeds than dirt.

You could tell the buildings for Janesville were expanded without much of a plan. The gym, cafeteria, and school were in one big building and two housing units sat right next to it. There was a small courtyard, and you could tell that these three were the original prison when it was first built because they all had matching, faded bricks.

Between the buildings were sidewalks that spidered out to other, newer buildings. The newer housing units were done well and made out of brick, but the counselors' and therapists' offices were in these boxy mobile homes that looked like they had a flat tire and leaned a little to one side. Somebody told me that the ground underneath, like, shifted and sank after they were set up, so that's why they looked like shit.

Septermber 7, 2010 7:10 PM

I got to live in Amelia B. When you walked into each living unit, you had to decide left, right or up, kinda like a normal apartment complex. Each newer cottage had an A and B unit on the first floor and a D and C unit on the second floor. They all looked the same with eight rooms in a circle around a living room. There was a shower room and a laundry area and a TV. That was about it.

Our cottage was named after Amelia Earhart, and the other main cottage was Eleanor cottage for Eleanor Roosevelt. The first two cottages built were condemned before I got there because the state didn't have the money for a new roof, and they caved in and shit. I don't know how they had enough money to build new ones but not take care of the old or at least tear them down.

Faith lived with me on Amelia B, and Regina live on Amelia D. Amelia A was used as a confinement area when somebody got in trouble, so nobody lived there; they just had sleepovers on occasion.

We'd have to walk between the condemned Harriet Tubman and Betsy Ross cottages any time we were going to school or dietary or rec. One of the windows for Betsy Ross was missing the glass but still had a metal screen, so we couldn't get in. Or, maybe it was so the raccoons couldn't get out. Those little critters, legit, had the run of the place.

School was six, hour long periods cut in half by lunch. We had the main four subjects plus gym and keyboarding. Even though it was just bitches locked up together, most people didn't want to sweat during gym. I think the teacher gave up years ago and was happy if the girls walked for more than half the period in a circle.

When I'd ask, Mr. Rivers would give me a soccer ball, and I'd kick it down the middle of the gym with somebody else who wanted to. Sometimes, we'd play a two person soccer match where one person was the shooter and someone else was a goalie. We'd try to hit an area on the wall, then we'd switch to do the same thing. We'd play best out of five games, but we had to pause when girls were walking past.

We never really got a full court game going because it just meant one of us would have to run faster than the other person to get a breakaway at the goal. That and the ball would regularly get loose and/or hit the walking girls which could turn into a regular bitch fit.

It didn't take long before I just walked in circles with the rest.

September 10, 2010 8:25 PM

This big bitch, Veronica, ran Janesville like it was her job. She made people, including the staff, call her VEE-ro because it was her street name or some shit.

On top of literally being twice my size, I mean this bitch was way over two hundred pounds and could have played pro basketball or something. On top of that, Ve-ro had these long ass nails that other girls swore she would sharpen against her dorm room walls.

She used those things like daggers. If somebody wasn't giving her what she wanted, she'd cozy up to them and grab their underarm next to the armpit until she drew blood. We all knew she did it, but Ve-ro would act hurt and offended and deny it.

If you really pissed Ve-ro off, she'd find an opportunity to slice you right behind your left ear. Always the left because that represented Ve-ro's gang. She was super slick with it because no one ever really officially caught her.

Every once in a while, Ve-ro would have to back it up because some bitch wouldn't like being sliced. Ve-ro was undefeated in all the fights she had, at least while I was there.

I only needed to experience Ve-ro's persuasiveness one time. I asked Regina what the deal was because her and Ve-ro went to the same school on the outside. Regina said Ve-ro was the real deal and had an army of brothers and uncles who'd throw a dude off a bridge if he crossed Ve-ro.

Warning received.

That shit ended when Ve-ro slashed across a security supervisor's face.

The S.S. was trying to hurry us through the dietary. Ve-ro was yucking it up and taking her sweet time. The S.S. gave her a one minute warning and took her tray from her. When Ve-ro refused to leave, the S.S. had two of her goons drag Ve-ro out and to her room.

After a cooling off period, S.S. Millars went to see if Ve-ro was ready to get with the program. The answer was *no*.

Ve-ro launched at the S.S.'s face, scratching that bitch raw. The warden ordered Ve-ro be put in restraints on her belly on a bed. While they had her in there, a couple of officers clipped her nails.

I got out shortly after that, so I don't know if that's how Ve-ro got her manicures from that point forward or if it was, like, a one time thing.

September 14, 2010 7:40 PM

Everybody had to go to some sort of therapy group after school on most days. Since my charges were drug related, I got enrolled in a drug group that would have been so much more entertaining if we were high. The therapist mumbled through lessons straight out of some workbook, and we had to write down our thoughts on every page. Then, the therapist would ask us to share, and everyone would stare at the floor hoping not to be called on.

If that shit didn't drive everyone who left Janesville to get so stoned they forgot the experience, I don't know what would.

About half-way through the group, our regular therapist got joined by some young intern. I could tell the intern was up too late studying most nights because even she had a hard time staying awake through the groups. I totally caught her bobbing her head on at least two occasions.

The food was decent, Charlie. Usually two or three of us got to work with the dietary staff to prep, serve and cleanup the food. On days when the meals weren't quite top notch, we'd make sure to put a big tub of hot sauce out to give the food some flavor.

The highlight was hamburger day when we had real ground beef. Mr. Aspen would show us how to mix spices and onions and garlic into the meat. We'd smoosh things together with our hands and use a circle plastic cookie cutter to mold the meat into burger shape.

Grilling those greasy burgers made the whole institute happy because you could smell it everywhere on grounds.

I really enjoyed the time in the kitchen because it reminded me of times in the diner with TJ. I almost felt like a little kid again.

September 16, 2010 8:05 PM

At some point, the fear of being in prison kinda faded away, and the time turned into, like, a summer camp experience. We were all fucked up, so no one really made fun of anybody else, and we bonded over being stuck in a bad place together.

Unlike the county, I didn't have to pair up with an older girl for protection. Some of the girls did date. Some of the girls firmly said they were only into dudes. And some girls, like me, appreciated a little attention and were willing to blur the lines while they were locked up.

The girls enjoyed flirting and teasing some of the younger male guards. The guards didn't know how to react. I think they thought some of us were hot, but looking the wrong way at a girl could get you fired or thrown in jail yourself. So, the boys mostly just flushed and told us to change the subject.

I didn't like making a big, public show out of flirting with the guards. I'd usually pick off the older, daddy figure guys that most of the other girls weren't paying attention to anyway. I don't know if I was flirting, but I'd just talk to them and ask them questions and get to know them.

I think most of the staff felt sorry for us being locked up so young, and people we'd buddy up to would let us out of our rooms for a longer time, bring us food like spicy chips, and work it out for us to hang out with other units that we liked.

I think we, like, mutually used each other. The guards wanted to have an easy day, so they'd give us what we wanted, and we didn't give them a hard time, so we'd keep the good times rolling.

That is until some bitch would fuck it up.

Most girls were on board, but there were always a couple, like Ve-ro, who couldn't leave the street life out on the streets. These girls had gang tattoos on their hands, arms, and neck and would talk in code using colors, numbers, and letters.

Every once in a while, this secret code would piss somebody off, and two or more girls would start screeching about this gang killed that person or that gang killed this person. It would always end in an ugly fight.

Girls would grab hair, tear clothes, scratch each other's faces, and even bite. You could almost guarantee that the girl who was losing the fight was gonna try to bite off a hunk of the other girl. Usually it was bites to the arms or leg that left a circular bruise for several weeks afterward.

Once, some crazy bitches were tearing at each other and got to grabbing and wrestling, and one bit off the top piece of the others ear. Her crazy ass didn't want to stop neither. She spit it on the ground and charged again.

The girl with her ear bit off had to rush to the hospital to get it sewed back on, but she had a jagged line scar in her ear that was never gonna heal right.

September 20, 2010 6:35 PM

School was boring as hell, and most of the teachers just made us do this quiet, independent, busy work. It usually didn't take long for us to get completely sidetracked and just start kicking it at our desks. Depending on the day, if we made it halfway through the period, the teachers would let it go.

One day, Maria just wasn't having it with Dr. Gil, and like five minutes into the period started harping on him for writing a nasty comment on her point card yesterday. Out of nowhere, Maria yells, "and this bitchass!" at Dr. Gil. Well, Gil bounces her from class.

Maria's all worked up, so she is gone for like half the period calming down. As soon as she gets back, she clears her throat loudly and says, "I have to pee."

Dr. Gil's having no more of her bullshit, so he tells her she's gonna have to wait. Maria doesn't protest, but two minutes later, she jumps out of her seat and drags her plastic chair into the hallway.

She screams for the whole school to hear, "This man made me pee myself!"

She keeps going with, "This motherfucker wouldn't let me go to the bathroom, so I peed myself. I want this motherfucker fired. I want this bitch's job."

Evidently, she runs into the principal's office, drenched in piss, dragging the dripping chair behind her. The principal had to coax her out of the school to change her clothes, but then, they let her crazy ass come to the next class with us.

That's fucked up, Charlie.

September 24, 2010 7:25 PM

I could tell you a million silly or fucked up stories about being locked up, Charlie. I really could. But to be honest, I really liked Janesville.

I went back again shortly after I was released because they sent me to live with Grandma Rosie. Because my mom was gonna be locked up for two to three years, they let our apartment go. So, Larry was staying right across the hall from me all the time.

I ended up calling this girl Riley who I'd met at Janesville, and her mom was cool with me staying with them.

It didn't take too long for my probation officer to catch up with me. Riley and her mom had to let me get taken back in, or they would have violated Riley's parole too for helping me out.

I'd told Riley and some of the other girls about Larry during a drug group session. This young intern, Ms.

Sprites, got us into some deep breathing and meditation and challenged us to think of the one thing we wanted to change, so we wouldn't want to do drugs anymore.

Some of the girls opened up and said that their parents or older brother or sister would have to get clean first. They were doing drugs to fit in with their family, Charlie.

Some said they did it because of the gang life or their friends and to drown out the violence in their neighborhoods.

I don't know what possessed me to come out and say Larry abused me. I think the fact that my life was so much easier than most of these girls problems. I wanted to say something that would put me on their level, so I'd fit in or something.

Charlie, shit got real after I opened up. Six other girls told the group about being raped or abused. We cried a little, and then, Ms. Sprites made us swear that we wouldn't talk about any of this outside of group.

I think that was a bonding experience that brought us all closer together. The mood of that group changed. It seemed like we'd all been through something brutal, and we were all stuck in Janesville together. It kind of created this tight bond.

We each felt a hurt and knew that the other people around us understood that hurt because they were hurting too. We were kinder to each other and more willing to stick up for each other and help the other person out.

As more and more groups happened and we opened up to share more details about how fucked up each of us was, we sort of became like each other's family. We trusted each other. We even probably loved each other.

September 27, 2010 7:25 PM

Now, who could that be this late at night, Charlie? Did you invite someone over without telling me, Big Boy?

Hey! HEY!!!

What's going on?!?

Let him go! He didn't do anything.

Don't touch me! Get your hands off me, bitch!

Charlie . . . CHARLIE!!! I'M SORRY, CHARLIE!!!

I'm so, so sorry, Charlie. I'm sorry . . .

September 30, 2010 10:00 AM

Dr. Charles P. Wallace and Rosa (Margarita) Gonzalez were taken into police custody and remanded to the county prison.

Dr. Wallace is charged with child abduction, human trafficking, statutory rape and custodial rape.

Ms. Gonzalez has outstanding warrants for running away from home, truancy, and failing to abide by the other terms of her parole.

The previous transcripts were found on Dr. Wallace's recording device and computer and were logged into evidence. They appear to be interviews between Dr. Wallace and Ms. Gonzalez dating back to October 9, 2009. This evidence will corroborate the illicit nature and the length of Dr. Wallace and Ms. Gonzalez's relationship.

End of report.

A special thanks to my dad for proof reading the first edition of this story. You've always been a source of wisdom and spurned me to dream bigger and reach farther.

There aren't words to express the gratitude I have for my writing partner, editor, wife, mother-of-my-children, and greatest source of joy. I'm forever fulfilled in simply knowing there's a spot to rest my head next to yours at the end of each day.

Thanks to the God of Providence whose good portions of manna continually sustain. Living in your guidance and statutes has given me more blessings that I could ever have dreamed.

Check out more from the author and book him for your next event by visiting our website.

www.widerlensproductions.com

Made in the USA
Lexington, KY
27 February 2018